"We have time for you to kiss me hello."

He drew her into his arms, bending his head to claim her mouth in a kiss that seemed to draw the very soul from her body.

Her lips opened to his as she felt his hands moving over her caressingly. The tan dress she wore was of a thin silky material, and through it she felt the heat of his body.

Lori clutched on to his shoulders as a familiar warmth began to invade her body; her head bent back as his kiss deepened to fierceness, his hands now fevered on her body, caressing her from breast to thigh. The zipper on her dress slowly slid down her spine, and Luke's hands followed the same path, curving her to him.

"Kitten, I love you," he groaned....

HARLEQUIN PRESENTS
by Carole Mortimer

These books may be available at your local bookseller.

For a free catalog listing all titles currently available,
send your name and address to:

Harlequin Reader Service
2504 West Southern Avenue, Tempe, AZ 85282
Canadian address: Stratford, Ontario N5A 6W2

CAROLE MORTIMER

subtle revenge

Harlequin Books

TORONTO • NEW YORK • LONDON
AMSTERDAM • PARIS • SYDNEY • HAMBURG
STOCKHOLM • ATHENS • TOKYO • MILAN

For
John and Matthew

Harlequin Presents first edition December 1983
ISBN 0-373-10651-3

Original hardcover edition published in 1983
by Mills & Boon Limited

CHAPTER ONE

LORI fought against the darkness, knowing what it would bring, knowing she couldn't face the nightmare again tonight. But it came anyway, bringing with it the desolation and loss she had never been able to accept.

The blackness cleared, giving way to a hazy greyness, as she saw her father's anguished face, her mother's grief, and finally Nigel's contempt.

'You should have told me,' he accused, his handsome face flushed.

Then came her own voice, crying out to him, pleading with him not to condemn her for the past.

He looked at her with cold blue eyes, his suit superbly tailored, his blond hair neatly styled. 'You know I can't marry you now.'

'No!' This time she cried out in earnest, thrashing about in the bed as she tried to reach the man in her dream, the man she loved. 'Nigel, I love you,' she begged. 'Don't leave me. Everyone has left me, my father, my mother—you can't leave me too!'

'Watch me,' he said in a chilling voice. 'Watch me walk out of the door and never look back. And next time you aim for respectability make sure you tell the man involved the truth about yourself. Because if you don't, I will.'

'No! Nigel, please,' she clutched on to his arm, feeling him flinch with the disgust with which he now held her, shaking her off. 'Nigel, you love me!'

'I *loved* Lori Parker, not Lorraine Chisholm. I could never love Lorraine Chisholm. Never!' he added vehemently.

She fell at his feet, sobbing, clutching at his legs as he tried to walk away. 'Nigel, don't go!' she sobbed.

'I have to.' He shook her off as if she were no more than a wearisome dog. 'No decent man in his right mind would want to have you as his wife.'

No decent man, no decent man ... As his wife, as his wife ...

'Lori, wake up!' Someone was shaking her shoulder. 'Lori, open your eyes. You're having a bad dream. Lori!' Again the shake on the shoulder, harder this time.

She forced herself through the realms of sleep, opening her eyes with effort, the greyness fading to give way to bright sunshine, the concerned face of her flatmate, Sally, gazing down at her worriedly.

'Are you all right?' Sally frowned. 'You were screaming so loud I thought someone was attacking you!'

Lori raised herself up on her elbows, pushing the red-gold hair back from her face, blinking long lashes over shadowed brown eyes. 'I should be so lucky,' she said ruefully. 'Just a nightmare.'

Sally moved back with a shrug, sitting on the single bed across from Lori's. 'It sounded real enough to me.'

'Nightmares always do,' Lori threw back the covers and swung her long legs to the floor. 'They always seem very real too, that's why they're so frightening.'

Sally stood up, a small, slightly plump girl with straight blonde hair down to her shoulders. 'This one sounded a real horror story,' she grimaced.

'It was.' Lori stretched with feigned nonchalance. 'But I've forgotten what it was about now,' she lied, knowing that particular horror would never leave her.

'You have?' Sally seemed doubtful too.

'Mm.' Lori stood up, padding over to the dressing-table to take her clean underwear from the top drawer. She was a tall girl, five feet eight inches in her bare feet, and the masculine pyjamas made her look slimmer than ever, and if it weren't for the rich cloud of red-gold hair that framed her beautiful face she could almost have looked boyish. Without her make-up she looked younger than her twenty-four years, her lashes naturally long and dark, her eyes a deep rich brown, her nose small and straight, her mouth a perfect bow, although she smiled little. She was aware of the fact that men were attracted to her combination of fiery appearance and icy manner, although very few of them ever got further than the first date.

'Then you won't remember who Nigel is?' Sally queried softly.

'Nigel?' She froze, then quickly regained her composure, concentrating deeply on finding the green bikini briefs that matched the bra she had already found. 'Nigel who?' she mumbled.

'I was hoping you could tell me that.' Her friend and flatmate eyed her curiously. 'You kept calling out his name in your sleep.'

'But I don't know anyone called Nigel.' She had found the bikini briefs now, but her bent head afforded her a certain amount of protection against Sally's curiosity.

'Maybe you do, maybe you just think——'

'Sally!' she slammed the drawer shut with force. 'I'm sure I would know whether or not I know anyone called Nigel—and I don't!'

'Sorry.' The other girl looked abashed.

'No,' Lori sighed deeply, 'I'm the one who's sorry. I think—I think the nightmare must have upset me more than I realised.' She looked at the other girl pleadingly.

'They do take it out of you, don't they,' Sally agreed

eagerly, as anxious as Lori to forget the subject now that she had seen how much it was upsetting her to talk about it. 'It was probably thinking about Nikki's wedding that made you sleep restlessly.'

'Yes,' she said dully. 'I-I'll use the bathroom first, shall I?'

'Go ahead,' the other girl invited goodnaturedly.

Sally couldn't know just how right she was, it *was* Nikki's wedding that had brought on the nightmare. The three girls worked together in a law firm, not actually together, but they spent most of their breaks together. Today was the day of Nikki's wedding to Paul Hammond, the junior partner of the firm, and also Nikki's boss, and what no one else could possibly realise was that five years ago next week should have been Lori's own wedding day. If Nigel hadn't walked out on her!

Nigel Phillips, heir to the Phillips fortune, junior partner in his father's law firm where Lori had been employed five years ago. His father had bitterly disapproved of Lori from the start, and it had been he who supplied the information that had driven Nigel and herself apart. She had believed that after all that time her past couldn't catch up with her, but as soon as Nigel learnt the truth about her he had broken their engagement, had cancelled the wedding. She had never fully recovered from the way he had let her down, and even though five years had passed August was still a traumatic month for her.

When Nikki had told her the date of her wedding and asked her to be a bridesmaid, her first instinct had been to refuse, and then her pride had made her say yes. Nigel might have made her wary of men, of becoming involved, but she couldn't let him influence her life in any other way. Nikki would have been deeply hurt if she had refused, but she had paid for her determination to go to the wedding with a series of the recurring nightmares that had plagued her the last five years. Last night had been the worst, though, refusing to be shaken off as she sometimes managed to do. Poor Sally must have wondered what on earth was happening!

'It's all yours.' She came out of the bathroom ten minutes later, a towel wrapped around her wet hair. Nikki had offered to take her to the hairdressers' with Sally and herself, but as her hair always reverted to the fluffy red-gold cloud she had known it was a waste of time and effort, preferring to wash and style it herself.

'I'm off now,' Sally called out a few minutes later, dressed in casual denims and a blouse, the pale green dresses they were to wear at Nikki's parents' house. 'I'll see you soon.'

'Okay.' Lori went through to the lounge, similarly dressed, her hair partly dry. 'And don't let Nikki get nervous and change her mind,' she teased, still looking a little strained.

'Are you joking?' Sally grinned. 'It took her months to catch the poor unsuspecting man.'

It was true. Nikki had mooned about over Paul for almost six months before he had plucked up the courage to ask her out. His proposal had been a little quicker in coming, only four months, and Nikki had arranged the wedding at top speed before he changed his mind.

'That poor, unsuspecting man happens to worship the ground Nikki walks on,' Lori said dryly. 'It seems incredible to me that the two of them had been in love with each other for months but neither thought the other one was interested,' she shook her head.

'That's the English for you!' Sally laughed before leaving.

Lori didn't remember guarding her own feelings
when she was younger, had never pretended to be
anything but completely in love with Nigel. It was
different now, now she was wary about caring for
anyone, and only Sally and Nikki had become good
friends over the last four years, since she had begun
working for Ackroyd, Hammond, and Hammond.
Ackroyd had been long dead, the senior Mr Hammond
was retiring in the near future, and the younger Mr
Hammond was Paul. Several other lawyers worked for
the firm too, but they weren't partners.

The elder Mr Hammond was Lori's boss, a big bluff
man who couldn't have been happier about his son
marrying Nikki. If only Charles Phillips could have felt
the same way about his son marrying his secretary!
Then there would have been no delving into the past,
no opening of old wounds, and now she might have
been Nigel's wife, might even have his children. That
had been Charles Phillips' worry, of course, not so
much her being Nigel's wife, but the fact that his
grandchildren would have Chisholm blood in their
veins.

She leant her head weakly against the dressing-table
mirror, letting its coolness soothe her. Normally she
didn't think of Nigel for days at a time, but today he
wouldn't be put from her mind. He had been ten years
her senior, had seemed experienced and sophisticated to
her awestruck gaze. When he had shown an interest in
her too she had been ecstatic, little realising that her
fragile beauty and obvious fascination made her an easy
victim to such a man. But Nigel had seemed to surprise
himself by falling in love with her, and had asked her to
marry him only a few weeks after their first evening
together.

All Nigel's family had been horrified by his choice of

bride—his snobby mother, his outraged father, and last his bitchy young sister Margot. But at least Margot had called her a gold-digger to her face. Charles Phillips had been much more underhand, producing his trump card only a week before the wedding.

Lori had stood and watched Nigel as the love drained from his eyes, while his face tightened with contempt, and in that moment her own hate had begun, mainly for Charles Phillips, but also for Jacob Randell, the man who had vindictively ruined her life in the first place, the reason for her father's early death, her mother's unhappy years before she too died prematurely.

She looked at herself in the mirror, seeing the thin face, the high cheekbones, but noticing none of the arresting beauty, the brown eyes seeming to have a golden ring around the iris, giving them a curiously cat-like appearance. She was as slender as a model, had the sort of figure that showed clothes well, although she considered herself too thin when undressed, her hips and waist were very narrow, her legs long and slender, her breasts small and uptilting.

Still, she wouldn't be the one being looked at today. Nikki would be the cynosure of all eyes. And so she should be, every girl deserved to be the belle of the ball on her wedding day!

Lori finished drying her hair and applying her make-up, determinedly not giving Nigel another thought. She had to be at Nikki's in an hour, and she didn't have the time to think of anything but getting ready for that.

All was chaos at the bride's house, Mrs Dean sure that the flowers weren't going to arrive on time, Mr Dean having locked himself in his study out of the way, much to his wife's annoyance. Lori telephoned the florist, something no one else seemed to have thought of, apparently, ringing off to assure the bride's mother that the flowers were on their way right now.

'Thank goodness you've arrived!' Nikki grabbed her, pulling her into her bedroom. 'Do something with my hair!' she wailed.

Lori frowned. 'What's wrong with it?' It looked perfectly all right to her.

'Nothing now, but look!' Nikki picked up the veil and put it on her head, instantly flattening the feathered style of her black hair. 'I forgot to take the headdress to the hairdressers so that they could work around it, and now I look a mess!' Tears filled her deep blue eyes.

'You don't look a mess at all,' Lori soothed her friend. 'It only needs a little restyling, this bit brought forward more and this bit smoothed out,' she suited her actions to her words, not making any drastic changes, just bringing the feathered fringe forward so that it was visible when the veil was put in place.

Nikki's eyes shone with happiness now instead of tears. 'I knew I could rely on you!'

Lori smiled. 'That's what chief bridesmaids are for. And talking of bridesmaids, where's Sally?' she frowned.

'Still at the hairdressers,' Nikki grimaced.

'What are they doing to her, giving her a transplant?' Lori derided.

'I hope not,' Nikki groaned. 'Her hair is already so thick it's taking twice as long as mine to dry! I came back to help Mum, but I wish I hadn't bothered!' she sighed.

'It's a bit chaotic, isn't it?' Lori laughed.

'Don't underestimate, Lori, it's bedlam! I wish now that we'd eloped!'

Lori laughed lightly. 'I'm sure every bride wishes the same thing before the wedding. But just wait until you see the photographs. It will be something to remember the rest of your life.'

'Mum keeps saying the same thing,' Nikki grimaced. 'I just wish it were all over.'

'Enjoy it,' Lori encouraged gently. 'It's a special day in your life, Nikki. Savour every minute of it.'

Her friend gave her a strange look, shrugging as some of the tension left her. 'You're right,' she nodded. 'This is my wedding day to Paul, why worry about the fact that Mum is having hysterics in the kitchen, Dad is locked in his study causing the hysterics, and the flowers haven't arrived!'

'Ah, now, the latter I can help you with,' Lori smiled. 'I've just seen the van from the florists pull up outside.'

Nikki rushed to join her at the window. 'Thank heavens for that!' she sighed her relief. 'That's one crisis over. Do you think Paul's buttonhole arrived safely?' she added worriedly.

'It was coming from the same florist, wasn't it?' Lori waited for her friend's nod of confirmation. 'Then I'll just go down and ask the lady if she went to Paul's first.'

'Why didn't I think of that?' Nikki said ruefully.

Lori gave a happy laugh at her friend's almost dazed expression. 'Because you're too excited to think of anything but being Paul's wife.'

'Yes,' Nikki gave a dreamy smile. 'I can't tell you how much I love him, how I'm longing to be married to him.' She blushed prettily. 'We've waited, you know, Lori.'

'I do know.' Lori squeezed her friend's hand. 'And that's also what makes today so special. The permissive society and equal rights in bed for women are okay, but there's nothing quite like a virginal bride.'

'Will you be——' Nikki broke off in embarrassment. 'I'm sorry, I shouldn't have asked that.'

'That's all right,' Lori dismissed huskily. 'I am, and I will be—if I ever find the right man.'

'Oh, you will,' her friend said with certainty. 'You're too beautiful for the male population to ignore. I'm just glad Paul goes for black hair instead of redheads!'

Lori gave a throaty laugh. 'I'd better go and check with the florist before she leaves.'

She found the middle-aged lady in the kitchen helping Mrs Dean drown her sorrows in a glass of sherry. Lori got confirmation about Paul's buttonhole before leaving them to it.

'I think your mother has decided to get drunk and let everyone take their chances,' she told Nikki laughingly when she got back upstairs.

'That's all I need!' her friend groaned. 'And I thought she would be the calm one.'

'Mothers aren't supposed to be calm on their daughter's wedding day, they're supposed to cry a lot,' Lori teased. 'Now isn't it time you changed into your dress? You don't want to be cruel and keep Paul waiting at the church.'

'It's getting awfully late,' Nikki frowned. 'I wonder where Sally is?'

'Now don't start panicking about Sally,' Lori instructed firmly. 'She'll be here, even if she has to leave with her hair still wet.'

'That's what I'm afraid of!'

'Well, don't. You'll see, it will all work out.'

And it did. Mr Dean finally decided to come out of the study and change into his suit, Mrs Dean put on the pretty flowered suit she was to wear, and Sally arrived in good time to help Nikki change.

'You look beautiful!' Lori kissed the glowing bride

warmly on the cheek, before they went downstairs to the cars waiting to take them to the church.

'We'll see you in a few minutes,' Sally squeezed Nikki's hand as Mr Dean came into the room.

The two bridesmaids were wearing identical pale green dresses, with small puff sleeves, a fitted bodice, gathered waist and flowing skirt to the floor, the tiny white roses in their hair matching the small posies they carried.

'I love weddings,' Sally grinned as they drove to the nearby church in the white Rolls-Royce.

'This one is certainly very beautiful,' Lori nodded, her hair looking a deeper red against the pale green gown.

'Maybe it will prompt Dave to propose,' the other girl said wistfully of the man she had been seeing the last two months.

Lori gave her a sharp look. 'Do you think he might?'

'No,' Sally laughed. 'But I live in hope.'

It was a beautifully warm day, the sun shining brightly, birds singing in the nearby trees. Lori felt herself get caught up in the occasion despite herself, and when Nikki arrived at the church on her father's arm she could have cried at the other girl's obvious happiness.

As was usual in churches it felt cold once they were inside, and Lori repressed a shiver as she and Sally followed Nikki and her father down the aisle, although the church looked completely different from when they had come here for the rehearsal earlier in the week. White flowers decorated the altar and sides of the church, and the whole place had a lighter, happier appearance.

Lori took Nikki's bouquet as the service began, listening to the beauty of the words of the service. And yet something else penetrated the subconscious of her mind, a prickling sensation down her spine, something that made her feel uncomfortable. She began to slowly look about her, sensing that someone was watching her. Everyone she looked at seemed intent on the bride and groom, or the service book in front of them. And yet she still sensed that there were eyes on her, still felt that uncomfortable sensation down her spine.

And then she saw him!

She looked hastily away again, and yet the man's face stayed imprinted in her brain. He was seated next to Mrs Hammond, a tall dark man with piercing grey eyes, an arrogant slash of a nose, lean cheekbones, a thinned mouth, his powerful physique looking magnificient in the grey morning suit, the shirt snowy white, a man of possibly thirty-eight, thirty-nine years of age.

She glanced back at him, finding those curiously light grey eyes still on her—and making no pretence of doing anything else. At twenty-four she was confident enough of her own attraction not to blush, meeting that arrogant gaze squarely for several seconds before slowly turning away. Those few seconds had given her chance to notice several other things about the man, like the sprinkling of grey in the darkness of his hair at his temples, the hardness of the grey eyes, the cynical twist to that almost sensual mouth.

His mouth quirked mockingly as she began to turn away, and for a moment her eyes widened. How dared he look at her so insolently! There were high wings of colour in her cheeks as she turned back to face the altar, but it was because of anger, not embarrassment, that her eyes sparkled like a cat's. Rude, arrogant man!

And what was he doing sitting next to Ruth Hammond? Paul didn't have a brother, she knew that, and his cousins had acted as ushers. But there he sat, with Ruth and Claude Hammond, almost like visiting royalty!

And he was still watching her, damn him! She didn't need to turn to know those grey eyes were still watching her, could feel the man's presence with ominous clarity. Ominous . . .? Now why should she have chosen a word like that? She had become adept, over the years, at putting down the wolves—even the apparently lethal kind, as this man appeared to be. He didn't frighten her, and if he chose to follow up this single-minded interest he seemed to have in her he would find out that he didn't attract her in least.

He was there again while the photographs were being taken, standing on the very edge of the crowd watching them, those light eyes still fixed on Lori. He seemed very tall out here in the sunlight, his hair pure black now, no grey distinguishable, his legs long and straight in the grey trousers, the jacket to the suit fitting snugly across his wide shoulders.

Lori's head was back proudly, her hair a red-gold cloud in the light breeze, her eyes the colour of honey in the sunlight.

'Luke!' Paul called out. 'Luke, come and join us.'

'Not me,' the man with the grey eyes spoke out lazily, his voice deep and controlled, the sort of voice that commanded attention.

'Oh, come on, Luke,' Paul cajoled.

'Yes, come on, Luke,' Nikki joined in the pleading, holding out her hand.

'Do I get to stand next to the chief bridesmaid?' he drawled, his gaze mocking as he saw Lori's mouth tighten.

All the guests laughed—with the exception of Lori. And Jonathan Anderson, the best man. Jonathan was one of the junior lawyers in the firm of Ackroyd, Hammond and Hammond, and he had been trying, unsuccessfully, to date Lori for the last six months. His arm tightened possessively about her waist as they stood in the group for the photograph, moving closer to her.

'Well, do I?' Luke mocked.

Lori was breathing heavily, hating the way this man was humiliating her in front of all these people. She didn't like attention drawn to her, a relic from the past, and she would never forgive this man for causing all the eyes to be on the both of them.

'Of course you do,' Nikki giggled.

'Then I accept.' He stepped forward, his movements fluid and forceful.

'Lucky Lori,' Sally murmured goodnaturedly. 'Where have you been hiding him, Nikki?'

Wherever it was, Lori wished he had stayed there. He had taken Jonathan's place now, his arm encircling her waist just as Jonathan's had, his body hard and unyielding, his arm implacable.

He smiled down at her as he felt her stiffen, a roguish smile, the coldness gone from his eyes, the cynicism from his mouth.

Lori pointedly ignored him, looking over at the photographer as he organised the bride and groom, the two bridesmaids, best man, and Luke in the photograph. A disgruntled Jonathan stood at Sally's side, and he grimaced as he caught Lori's gaze.

As the photographs continued to be taken Luke remained at her side, his hand never moving from the slender curve of her waist, accepting her haughtiness, but unaffected by it.

'Bride and groom only now,' the photographer requested briskly, having done this so many times now it was rather boring for him.

His words were all the encouragement Lori needed, and she evaded that confining arm to slip away into the crowd, noting with satisfaction as the man called Luke was waylaid by Claude Hammond. He had obviously intended talking to her, and as she didn't like anything about him she had no wish to talk to him.

Nevertheless, his silent admiration continued at the reception, his fixed gaze starting to become embarrassing. He had no right to look at her like that, to mentally strip her with his eyes. And they were such all-seeing eyes, slightly narrowed, their expression enigmatic.

'Damned cheek!' Jonathan muttered at her side.

Lori continue to smile at him, taking the glass of champagne he held out to her. She didn't need any explanation as to the reason for his anger, the resentful glances he was still shooting at the dark-haired man across the room spoke for him.

'Who the hell is he?' he snapped, standing in front of her and effectively blocking her view of the room behind him.

She shrugged. 'I have no idea. A friend of the Hammonds', I suppose,' she infused uninterest into her voice, although her own curiosity about the man was quite strong.

'Mm,' Jonathan nodded. 'Nikki seems to know him too,' he added questioningly.

'She's never mentioned him.'

'Hm,' Jonathan said again, turning to look at Luke, who was now deep in conversation with Paul. 'Interesting-looking chap.'

Dangerous, she would have said. Ominous *and* dangerous? Considering she had never even spoken to the man he had made a deep impression on her!

She might not have spoken to him, but he had said enough with those eyes, was still saying it!

'Like to dance?' Jonathan offered.

'Thank you,' she nodded, smiling up at him.

Jonathan was a dear, she knew he was, and yet something held her back from going out with him. He reminded her too much of Nigel, the same blond hair, the same good looks. The same determination to succeed! She knew that, like Nigel, he would never think of taking Lorraine Chisholm for his wife.

They moved well together, both tall, the red cloud of Lori's hair drawing attention to the beauty of her face, a beauty Jonathan seemed fascinated by, for he gazed down at her with admiring eyes.

Lori chuckled as they continued to dance together as each successive melody was played. 'I think we're supposed to change partners, or at least take a break occasionally,' she teased.

'I know,' he muttered. 'But if we stop that man called Luke is going to ask you to dance, and I don't intend giving him the chance.'

She frowned, glancing round. Yes, there were those steady grey eyes on her still, more searching now, as if something about her puzzled the man. Heavens, he couldn't have recognised her, could he! She felt her panic rising, and then dismissed it. It wasn't possible that after all this time someone should recognise her. Charles Phillips had only discovered the truth because he had had someone delve into her past; she bore little resemblance to the bewildered young girl she had been all those years ago.

No, it couldn't be because he recognised her, her years of disguise had been too effective. Maybe he was just trying to unnerve her. Sad to say, he had succeeded!

'Let's sit this one out,' she requested stiffly of Jonathan.

'Oh, but——'

'If he asks, Jonathan, I shall simply refuse,' she told him haughtily.

'You will?' he still looked uncertain.

'Yes, I will.' She moved out of his arms, turning to walk into the hard wall of a masculine chest.

Strong hands came up to steady her, grasping her upper arms, the fingers long and tapered, a hidden strength within them. 'Lori,' drawled a deeply familiar voice.

She had known it was him the second before impact with his chest, had detected the slight smell of his aftershave, had vaguely seen the strong line of his square jaw.

'Thank you—Luke,' she nodded coolly, making to move out of his grasp. His hands remained, not hurting, but not gentle either.

'Dance with me,' he requested huskily.

'I——'

'We were just about to go through to the buffet,' Jonathan cut in purposefully, taking one of Lori's hands and putting it in the crook of his arm. 'If you'll excuse us,' he gave the other man a smug smile before moving away. 'Saved by the bell—or in this case, food,' he muttered as they followed the stream of people into the room that contained the buffet dinner.

'You aren't very subtle, Jonathan,' she smiled at his undoubted jealousy of the other man.

'With that type subtlety doesn't work,' he scowled. 'I can be subtle if I have to be.'

Lori knew that; she had once gone to court with him when his own secretary had been on holiday. She had been amazed at the change that had come over him, amazed and dismayed. He had been totally remorseless in his attack on the defendant, reminding Lori of another courtroom, another lawyer. Jacob P. Randell. Just the name made her shiver!

She saw the man called Luke several times during the evening, mostly with the Hammonds, once or twice with Sally on the dance floor, the latter blushing prettily as he spoke to her, a fact Dave viewed with a scowl on his petulantly handsome face. Not that Lori thought a little jealousy would do that young man any harm—he was altogether too sure of Sally for her liking, and she feared for her friend's deeply committed love.

But Luke didn't approach her again, pointedly so, seeming to move away if she should happen to approach the group he was talking to, his gaze always fixed firmly in the opposite direction if she should unavoidably look at him.

She knew what he was doing, of course, and her anger towards him grew. He surely didn't think she was idiot enough to become interested in him merely because he was suddenly ignoring her? She had stopped playing those sort of games years ago, if she had ever played them, and she certainly wasn't going to be drawn into that sort of trap.

'Dance, my dear?' The elderly Mr Hammond, her own personal boss, stood in front of her, his hair still as dark as his son's, his step still as youthful, although he perhaps looked a little tired lately. The excitement of the wedding, she supposed. Lori had been his personal secretary for the last two years, and although she might have been a little young for the promotion she had made sure he never regretted giving her that chance.

'I'd love to.' She moved gracefully into his arms, finding he moved easily across the dance floor despite his portly figure. 'The wedding went beautifully, Mr Hammond.'

He looked pleased. 'I thought so.'

Lori knew that the Deans and the Hammonds had

paid jointly for their children's wedding arrangements, the Rolls-Royces and this costly reception, that Ruth Hammond had insisted her only son should be married in style. Poor Nikki and Paul would much rather have had a much quieter wedding, but to please the two mothers they had agreed to this extravagant affair.

'Nikki looked beautiful,' the elder Mr Hammond said with pride. 'I couldn't have chosen better myself.'

Nikki had been floating on cloud nine all through the wedding, and Paul wasn't far behind her. The happy couple had eyes only for each other, which, after all, was the way it should be.

'And now, with your permission, I'll pass you on to my young friend.' Mr Hammond had stopped dancing while Lori was so deep in thought, releasing her. 'I know he's been longing to meet you all day. Luke . . .?' he prompted with a fatherly smile.

Lori viewed her tormenter of the day with angry eyes, the gold around the irises seeming to make them glow. Mr Hammond viewed the two of them with an indulgent smile, obviously very pleased with himself.

'Lori?' Luke mocked her.

She swallowed her anger. He was a friend of the Hammonds', how much of a friend she didn't know, but she could hardly be impolite to him in front of her employer.

'Very wise,' he taunted as she moved stiffly in his arms to the music, the elder man having rejoined his wife at their table.

'I beg your pardon?' She bent her head back to look at him, at once wishing she hadn't, finding he was much too close. He was so close she could see the exact smoky grey colour of his eyes, the thickness of his dark brows and lashes, the fullness of his mouth, the lower lip sensually so as he gazed back at her.

'I could be an important friend of Claude's,' he drawled in answer to her question.

Lori turned away, angry that he could read her thoughts so easily. And did he have to hold her so tightly?

'Yes, I have to,' he told her softly.

She blinked up at him dazedly. Could he read her every thought, for goodness' sake!

'More or less,' he derided, smiling as she gasped. 'It's those eyes of yours,' he continued softly. 'At first they just look brown, then you notice that the gold circles make them change colour with your mood. Like right now. You're angry, your eyes have gone the colour of honey. You have the eyes of a cat, Lori,' he laughed throatily. 'Like the sleek ginger tabby I had as a child. I loved making that cat purr, Lori.'

'How fascinating,' she said with saccharine sweetness.

His thumb-tip moved rhythmically over her wrist. 'You aren't as calm as you sound,' he mocked, his thumb stopping pointedly on her fast pulse. 'Enigmatic like a cat too,' he murmured. 'Do you scratch like a cat too when cornered, little kitten?'

She looked at him with cold eyes. She knew his bold manner and rugged good looks would appeal to a lot of women, but for her he held no attraction. 'I never put myself in a position where I can be cornered, Mr— Luke. Although I've always admired the cat as a species.'

'So have I. Even more so now,' he drawled. 'But I think I would enjoy having you purr more than I would have you scratch me.'

Lori pulled away from him, taking exception to the innuendo this time. 'I never *purr*. Now if you'll excuse me, I think Nikki and Paul are about to leave.' She walked away, a tall graceful woman. It would have irked her immensely to know that several of the people watching her thought she had the sensuous grace of a cat!

'Thank you for everything you did to help, Lori.' Nikki came over to hug her, ecstatically happy, looking very beautiful in the stunning lemon dress she had chosen to wear for the flight to Barbados. 'Hasn't it all been wonderful?' she glowed.

'Wonderful,' Lori nodded, kissing her friend warmly on the cheek. 'Now off you go and join your impatient bridegroom.'

'What are you going to do about poor Luke?' Nikki giggled, needing no champagne to make her intoxicated, although she had probably had some of the bubbly wine too. 'He's quite smitten, you know.'

Now was her chance to find out more about him. 'But, Nikki, wh——'

'Come along, darling.' Paul's arm came about his new wife's waist. 'Sorry to interrupt, Lori,' he kissed her on the cheek, 'but the car is waiting to take us to the airport.'

'Sorry, Lori,' Nikki looked regretful, 'but we'll talk when I get back,' she promised before she was pulled away by her husband.

Lori sighed her dismay. The new husband and wife were to be away for a month, so Nikki was going to be no help at all where the man called Luke was concerned.

'She's quite right, you know,' he spoke softly behind her, startling her. Although she didn't know why—he was starting to be her nemesis! 'I am smitten,' he looked down at her with serious grey eyes. 'So what are you going to do with me?'

'Nothing!' she snapped, turning away. 'Except ignore you.'

'I'm afraid I'm not very ignorable,' he derided softly.

Lori maintained a stony silence, watching as Nikki tearfully gave her bouquet of roses to her mother, and the two of them hugged each other tightly before Nikki got into the car with Paul.

'If she had thrown that bouquet,' Luke's voice was strangely close to her ear. 'I'd catch it for you. Because you're going to be the next bride, Lori. *My* bride.'

She couldn't keep her silence after red-flagwaving like that! 'Are you mad?' she rasped, turning to him fully as the bridal car drove away and the crowd began to wander back into the ballroom of this fashionable London hotel now that the bride and groom had left.

'I'm beginning to think I must be,' but he didn't sound too worried about it. 'But you are going to marry me, Lori.'

'I—Never!' she almost shouted, running to catch up with the other guests, sure that he was a madman.

She was going to marry him, indeed! She had hardly spoken to the man, let alone—He *was* mad!

'Lori, my dear,' Claude Hammond approached her, 'I'm glad to see you and Luke are getting on so well together.'

'Oh, but——'

'Brilliant man. Brilliant!'

That was high praise indeed, coming from this north-country man. Lori listened with more interest. If Claude Hammond said the man was brilliant then he must indeed be so. At what she had no idea.

'With a father like that he was bound to be outstanding,' Claude Hammond continued. 'I'm proud to know him.'

'A father like that?' Lori prompted.

'Mm, Jacob was the best.'

'J-Jacob . . .?' she echoed with a sickening jolt in her stomach. It couldn't be——

'Jacob Randell,' Claude explained jovially. 'Of course he made that one mistake with the Chisholm case, underestimated the man. But that was before your time.'

No, not before her time at all, she remembered it very well, both the case and Jacob Randell. He was a man with the ruthlessness of a viper, a cruelty that inflicted scars in his victims. And she remembered Michael Chisholm too. Her father . . .

CHAPTER TWO

THE court case had gone on for months—months and months, when both Lori and her mother had been as much in the public limelight as her father had. They had been hounded by photographers wherever they went. Even on the day her father had been buried . . .

'Of course it was a shame the case couldn't reach its proper conclusion,' Claude Hammond continued with a shake of his head. 'I'm sure Jacob would have got his conviction. Still, I mustn't bore you with history, my dear,' Claude smiled. 'Especially on a day like today. Old fogeys like Jacob and myself can't be of much interest to you.' He patted her hand. 'You go ahead and enjoy yourself. It's early yet.'

Lori gazed after him with widely shocked eyes. Luke Randell was the son of the man she hated most in the world, the man who had caused her father to take his own life, who had been responsible for her mother's subsequent failing health and prematurely young death, who had been the cause of all the misery in her life, including losing Nigel, the man she loved.

No one looking at her could have guessed quite the shock she had just received, the trauma. Her expression remained calm, her movements unhurried as she entered the door marked 'Ladies', but the memories suddenly crowded in on her.

Twelve years, twelve long miserable years, when her own and her mother's name was changed to Parker. But the change of a name couldn't eradicate the shame her mother felt, the fact that her husband had been accused of being a criminal, and that his suicide before he could be sentenced had seemed to confirm this.

For the next five years Lori had watched her mother shrivel up and die, had watched the life slowly fade from within her, her once happy carefree face no longer beautiful but ravaged with age, the pride she had taken in her youthful figure no longer there; she often did not even bother to dress at all towards the end. A heart attack, the doctor had diagnosed at her death at only thirty-eight, but Lori had known the real cause of death, and at seventeen she had sworn vengeance on Jacob P. Randell.

All her excellent capabilities as a secretary had been attained for the sole reason of eventually getting to work for Jacob P. Randell, of somehow being able to discredit him, of ruining him. She wasn't even sure how she had thought she could do that, she had just felt that if he had been so wrong about her father—and he had been wrong—that there had to be other cases he had been wrong about, cases where he had got a conviction merely to further his career.

Before she had even qualified she had learned that Jacob P. Randell had retired, and her plans for revenge were foiled before they had even begun.

But he had a son, a son she hadn't even known existed, a man who minutes ago had told her he intended marrying her! She hadn't liked him from the beginning, even when she had had no idea who he was, of the devastating effect his father had had on her life. Luke *Randell*—she could hardly believe it, not after all this time.

She had left the idea of vengeance far behind her, had buried the bitterness she had for the past, knowing it could never be undone, that it was much too late to

help her mother and father. But Nigel and herself——?
It was too late for them too!

'Lori, my dear,' Ruth Hammond entered the powder-room to join her on another of the velvet stools in front of the ornate mirrors. 'I thought for a moment you'd left without saying goodbye,' she smiled.

Lori gathered herself together with effort. 'I wouldn't do that, Mrs Hammond,' she returned the smile, only the strain in her eyes telling of her disturbed emotions.

She liked her employer's wife, found the other woman had a cryptic wit and a quite surprising sense of fun, despite her sometimes uncomfortableness with her husband's north-country bluntness. Being a southerner Ruth was a little more reserved, but her forthright husband believed in calling a spade a spade, sometimes with embarrassing repercussions. Lori found them an enchanting couple, and knew that they had a genuine affection for each other.

'Claude and I would like you to come to lunch tomorrow. Could you manage that?' Ruth raised finely shaped brows, still an attractive and energetic woman despite being sixty years of age. 'There'll just be the four of us,' she added encouragingly.

'Four of us?' Lori echoed softly.

'You, Claude and I—and of course, Luke,' Ruth added coyly.

If the last was supposed to be an incentive it had the opposite effect. 'I'm sorry,' Lori shook her head, 'I have to visit my aunt.'

A look of irritation crossed Ruth's perfectly made up face. 'Couldn't you do that some other time?'

'No, I'm afraid not.' Her Aunt Jessie, Great-Aunt Jessie, would never forgive her if she missed one of her visits. The old lady had put herself into a nursing home two years ago, treating the place more like a hotel than anything else. In fact, Lori often thought her aunt ran the old people's home instead of the Matron!

'Damn!' Ruth frowned. 'Luke is only with us for the weekend, then he's moving into his flat. Couldn't you come for tea instead?' she asked hopefully.

Once again Lori shook her head, glad she had a real excuse for refusing—if she hadn't Ruth would soon have worn her down. And she never, ever, wanted to see Luke Randell again; she hated him for the bitter memories he had evoked.

'I always spend the whole day with my aunt,' she said truthfully.

'Oh well, I don't suppose it can be helped,' Ruth murmured disappointedly. 'I did so want you to meet Luke.'

'I've already met him,' Lori said coldly.

'I meant away from the rush and bustle of the wedding. He's been in America for several years, and he seems to have lost contact with a lot of his friends. Of course, we've been friends of the family since Luke was a child. But I thought perhaps you—well, if you can't make it, you can't.' She stood up resignedly. 'Do come back and join the party, Lori.'

'In a moment,' she nodded. 'I just want to repair my make-up.'

Ruth smiled. 'You don't have much to worry about, you always look lovely. When you get to my age it becomes more than a repair job, it's a total remake!'

Lori joined in the laughter, but her own humour faded as soon as the door closed behind the other woman. She had a suspicion, more than a suspicion, that Luke Randell had made the request for her to be invited to the Hammonds'. She was friendly with the other couple, enjoyed talking to Ruth when she came to the office to visit her husband, but she had never been invited to their home before.

So Luke Randell had been in America the last few years. Probably reflecting in his father's undoubted glory, she thought bitterly.

Bitterness. It was something that she had tried to forget, especially after she had fallen in love with Nigel. After he had walked out of her life she had pulled herself together enough to move from the flat she had been renting, to get herself a new job as soon as possible. And she had tried not to let bitterness rule her life for a second time.

And now *Luke* Randell had suddenly appeared in her life, bringing back all the destructive memories, destroying the self-confidence she had built up over the years.

Well, she wouldn't let him destroy her! She was Lori Parker, not Lorraine Chisholm, was a very competent and trusted personal secretary to an important London lawyer, and no human reminder from the past was going to ruin that for her.

She would make her excuses to leave the wedding reception as soon as possible, and after that she would never have to see Luke Randell again.

'I thought you were going to hide in there all night, little kitten!'

She spun round to confront Luke Randell, finding him leaning against the wall, a suitable distance away, although obviously waiting for her. He pushed easily away from his lounging position, and Lori viewed him with new eyes as he walked confidently towards her.

On the surface he bore little resemblance to the man she remembered his father to be. His hair was black where his father's had been silver; he was taller than his father too, his body not tending towards flabbiness as the other man's had, his features vaguely similar, although much more strongly defined in the son, the ruthlessness not hidden behind a smooth charm in the younger man as it had been by his father's benign, often sympathetic, expression. That hidden ruthlessness had been turned on her father with vicious cruelty once Jacob P. Randell had him off his guard, twisting his words until even he didn't know what he was saying. It had been like watching a snake strike at an unsuspecting mouse, and her father's final agony had been the taking of his own life. His imminent conviction had been obvious, thanks to Jacob P. Randell.

The day after her father's death, away from prying eyes, Lori and her mother had read the letter her father had left for them. He had still claimed his innocence, although having already spent several months in a prison cell, he knew he couldn't stand the years that stretched ahead of him in the same way. He preferred to die rather than live in that degradation.

'Kitten?' Luke prompted, standing in front of her now, his eyes narrowed on her pale face.

Lori looked up at him, pulling herself back from the past, and Luke Randell's face swam back into focus. 'I wasn't hiding, Mr Randell,' ice dripped from her voice. 'Now if you'll excuse me . . .'

'No.'

She blinked up at him. 'No?'

'No.' His hand was firm on her arm, and he frowned deeply as she snatched away from him. He folded his arms across his chest. 'You've been running away from me all day,' he drawled, 'and up until now I've been letting you. I've finally caught up with you—and I'm not letting you get away. Why did you turn down Ruth's invitation for lunch tomorrow?'

Her mouth tightened, and she looked round for

Jonathan so that she could take advantage of his earlier offer of a lift home. 'I already have an engagement for tomorrow,' she told Luke Randall absently, unable to see Jonathan anywhere.

'Break it,' Luke instructed.

She looked at him scornfully. 'I don't do things like that, Mr Randall. My word is my bond. It's a family trait,' she added vehemently.

'Very commendable,' he drawled. 'But I would like to see my future bride tomorrow. Maybe we could discuss the wedding?'

She gave him a pitying glance. 'I think you've had too much champagne, Mr Randell.'

'Luke,' he encouraged softly. 'And when I decided to marry you I hadn't had any champagne.'

'When *you* decided, Mr Randell?' she deliberately used the formality. 'I thought it was supposed to be a joint decision?'

'It is,' he shrugged, his shoulders broad, the muscles ripping across his chest. 'You're just a little longer making your mind up than I am.'

'We only met today,' she scorned disbelievingly, wondering that even Jacob P. Randell's son should have so much arrogance.

'That's all it takes,' he dismissed.

Lori sighed, knowing she had to get away, and soon. Her search for Jonathan was becoming almost frantic. If she really lost her temper with this man there was no telling what she would say!

Luke noticed her preoccupation, and his mouth quirked into a smile. 'Kitten, I——'

'Don't call me that!' she shuddered, hating the intimacy of a pet name from this man. 'I don't like it. Ah, Jonathan!' she called to the other man as she finally spotted him. 'Goodbye, Mr Randell.' Just saying his name reminded her of exactly who he was—and the contempt and hatred she had for all his family.

No doubt a lot of women found him devastatingly attractive, would like his almost roguish behaviour, the promise of intimacy in his devilish grey eyes, but knowing what she did about him gave him no chance with her—even if his approach was the most original she had ever known! No doubt she was supposed to believe he really meant the marriage proposal, and would only find out if had all been a 'joke' once she had slept with him.

His narrow-eyed gaze levelled on Jonathan as the other man came towards them. 'Your young friend again,' he growled his displeasure. 'A boy-friend?'

'I—Yes.' She was sure Jonathan would forgive her that exaggeration. After all, he was just waiting for the day she said yes to one of his invitations.

'Your previous engagement for tomorrow?' Luke quirked one dark brow.

She was tempted to say yes, but Ruth might already have told him about the visit to her aunt. 'No.'

He nodded. 'I thought not. I'm not giving up on you, kitten,' he drawled confidently. 'The Jonathans of this world don't mean a thing to me. I doubt they mean anything to you either.'

Jonathan had almost reached them now, and Lori felt indignant on his behalf. He was a very good-looking man, not as dark as the devil like this man, but neither did he have his cold ruthlessness.

'Lori!' He had reached her side now, taking her hand in his, his pleasure at being with her evident. 'Mr Randell,' he greeted respectfully, obviously having learnt who the older man was, whose *son* he was. For the same reason Jonathan admired him Lori hated him.

'I'm ready to leave now, Jonathan,' she told him pointedly.

'Hm? Oh—oh yes,' he gave a light laugh. 'Nice to have met you, sir,' he shook Luke's hand strongly.

Lori felt a sense of satisfaction at the sudden tightness of Luke Randell's mocking mouth. Jonathan's 'sir' had been meant as a show of respect, nevertheless the other man didn't like it, obviously feeling his at least ten years' seniority over the other man, being somewhere in his late thirties.

'Likewise,' Luke drawled, the very faintest trace of a transatlantic accent discernible in his irony. He turned to Lori. 'We'll meet again,' was all he said to her, and yet she knew he meant it.

She met his gaze steadily for several seconds, seeing the determination in his jaw, the challenge in the light-coloured eyes as he waited for her reply. It sent a shiver of apprehension down her spine. She had been wrong about there being little similarity between father and son. The eyes, those grey steely eyes, were the same, containing a strange mixture of warmth and cruelty.

'I doubt it,' she snapped, nearing the end of her control, and looking to Jonathan to help her now. 'Ready?' she prompted him, her chin high, studiously avoiding looking at Luke Randell again.

'Of course,' Jonathan agreed readily.

Lori moved smoothly across the room at his side, unaware of the striking figure she made in the pale green dress, her movements graceful and fluid, her hair moving silkily as she walked.

She might have looked relaxed as she made her laughing goodbyes to the Hammonds, might have appeared calm as she followed Jonathan outside to his low sports car. But once she had sunk into the bucket-seat her breath left her in a hiss, her lower limbs felt trembly, her hands shook as she clenched them in her lap.

Jonathan noticed none of this as he climbed in beside her, his lean length fitting into the car from habit, his long legs only slightly cramped. 'Do you realise who that was?' he said excitedly, backing the car out of its parking space and accelerating into the busy traffic.

She might have known Jonathan would suffer from a case of hero-worship! Jacob P. Randell was set up as a prime example to all young lawyers, that one single blemish on his career when he had pushed the accused too far being forgotten at such times. Luke, as his son, came in for the same admiration.

'Yes, I realise,' she sighed, leaning her elbow against the window to put her hand up to her aching temple.

'Luke *Randell!*' he shook his head in disbelief. 'Fancy having the great Jacob to live up to!'

'I'm sure Mr Randell—Mr *Luke* Randell,' she defined with distaste, 'has more than lived up to his father's hopes for him.'

'He's a lawyer too, you know,' Jonathan was awestruck, not seeming to notice Lori's aversion to the subject.

She hadn't known, but it didn't come as any surprise to her. What else could the son of such a famous man do? And he would be good at it too, would have the same presence in court that his father had, would take to the stage as if born to it.

Jonathan glanced at her. 'I never knew there was a son, did you?'

'I never gave it a thought.' Which was true. The way Jacob P. Randell had broken her family apart, destroyed it, it had never occurred to her that he could possibly have a family of his own, that there were actually people who *loved* such a man.

'Mr Hammond has nothing but praise for him,' Jonathan continued.

'Yes,' she acknowledged, wondering how such an astute man could be so deceived.

'I wonder if——'

'Jonathan!' she cut sharply across his words. 'Do you think we could talk about something other than Luke Randell?'

A ruddy hue coloured his cheeks. 'Sorry. I was just—You're right, what am I doing talking about him when I have you alone at last?'

'I have no idea,' she mocked.

'Neither do I,' he grinned. 'Do I get invited in for coffee?'

'Sally——'

'Went off with her boy-friend hours ago. I think the air of romance got to them,' Jonathan added with a twinkle in his laughing blue eyes.

Lori laughed softly, beginning to relax once again. 'In that case, you do get invited in—for coffee.'

'What else?' he quipped with pretended hurt.

She smiled at him, wondering why she had never allowed him this close to her before. As a friend, she was sure, he could be a lot of fun. And she needed fun in her life at the moment, needed to erase a pair of piercing grey eyes from her memory. Along with all the other painful memories meeting Luke Randell had raked up!

'The wedding didn't introduce an air of romance in me,' she added teasingly.

'Just my luck!' Jonathan grimaced.

Sally and Dave weren't at the flat when they got in, so Lori knew they must have gone to Dave's flat instead. Dave was a local electrician, and Sally had met him at a party a couple of months ago. Unfortunately

Sally had fallen in love with him—unfortunately, because Dave's affections seemed to be less engaged. Much to Lori's embarrassment he had even made a couple of passes at her behind Sally's back, although not for anything would she hurt her friend by telling her so. She only hoped Sally wasn't going to get too hurt, had a feeling the relationship meant one thing to Sally and something else completely to Dave.

'Nice place,' Jonathan looked about the flat appreciatively. 'But then I knew you would have good taste.'

Lori looked over at him as he lounged in one of the armchairs. 'Did you indeed?' she said dryly, having changed from the long bridesmaid's dress into a silky dress, looking tall and slender.

He shrugged. 'Everything about you is—perfection.'

Her mouth quirked teasingly. 'How much champagne did you have today?'

'Not much,' he dismissed seriously. 'I don't need champagne to know how beautiful you are. Luke Randell thought so too,' he scowled. 'I should watch him, Lori, his sort play by their own set of rules.'

'I have a few rules of my own,' she told him stiffly.

'Oh?'

'Yes,' she bit out. 'I never go out with a man I detest.' Her eyes glittered her hatred.

'Hey, steady on——!'

'I think you should go now,' she cut across his embarrassed words. 'It's been a long day.'

'Yes, but—Okay,' he sighed as she saw her determined look. 'I don't suppose it would do any good for *me* to ask you out?'

She looked at his hopeful expression and her anger instantly faded, the hectic rise and fall of her breasts steadying. Jonathan could have no idea of her inner turmoil, of the deep shock she had received today. It had probably surprised him at the amount of vehemence the usually cool Lori Parker could display at a complete stranger.

If only Luke Randell had been a stranger, then she would merely have rebuffed his outrageous approach, would probably have forgotten about him by now. But she couldn't put him from her mind—and heaven knows she was trying to!

'Try me again on Monday,' she told Jonathan vaguely, wanting more than anything to be on her own for a while. And there was a good chance of her being alone all night. The single bed across from her own was often empty now.

He grimaced. 'I've heard that before. You've been putting me off for six months like that. I thought today I was finally making some impression.'

She was instantly contrite, smiling at him warmly. 'How about dinner on Monday?'

'You mean it?' He suddenly looked younger than his thirty years in his eagerness.

'I mean it,' she nodded.

'Really? I mean—well, I——'

'If you don't want to . . .'

'Don't you dare change your mind!' Jonathan stood up to grasp her arms. 'Don't you dare!' He kissed her hard on the mouth. 'Monday, eight o'clock. I'll call for you here. And no excuses!' He was whistling happily, if tunelessly, as he left.

Lori kept her mind a blank, refusing to question her sudden acquiescence to Jonathan, refusing to think of Luke Randell. Years of training, of having to bury her private pain, enabled her to succeed in doing exactly that, and her last worrying thoughts were of Sally and the number of nights she was spending with Dave.

CHAPTER THREE

SALLY still hadn't returned the next morning as Lori ate her solitary breakfast before getting herself ready for her visit to Aunt Jessie. Even at eighty years of age Aunt Jessie was a stickler for smartness, and Lori put on one of the suits she wore to work, a rust-coloured one contrasted with a cream blouse, the scarf-collar tied neatly at her throat. Her make-up was light, her hair brushed until it gleamed. Aunt Jessie wouldn't be able to fault her appearance today—as she often did! Aunt Jessie was her greatest critic, she had also been her one stability during the last twelve years.

'You're late,' the old lady snapped as Lori let herself into the tiny lounge her aunt shared with another woman, two small bedrooms and an even tinier kitchen going off this main room. The boarders of the home lived in pairs in these tiny self-contained flats within the home, although there were several big lounges too where they could all get together, and unless the boarders had visitors and preferred to cook for themselves, they all ate together in the main dining-room on the ground floor.

'Sorry,' Lori accepted the criticism with a smile, and gave her aunt the plant she had brought with her.

The flat was like a small greenhouse, and poor Mrs Jarvis, the woman who shared the flat, had to put up with it, whether she wanted to or not. Luckily the other woman liked plants, but even if she hadn't the autocratic Aunt Jessie wouldn't have parted with one of her beloved plants. Lori could still remember the shock

43

on the Matron's face the day Aunt Jessie had moved in two years ago as Lori unpacked the car full of potted plants. Aunt Jessie had consistently refused to give up her greenery ever since, and now the Matron, and all the other staff, had become accustomed to walking through a jungle when they came into this flat.

The old lady eyed Lori over the top of her pink-framed spectacles, her faded blue eyes still lit with a quick intelligence, her hair snowy white, her lined face still possessing some of her great-niece's beauty, and her movements still spritely, despite the fact that she suffered quite badly from rheumatism.

'What's happened to you, girl?' she asked in her abrupt voice, the short-sharpness of her manner belied by the affectionate twinkle in her light blue eyes.

Lori returned that affection. No one would ever believe her great-aunt was eighty years old—she looked as if she would go on for ever. And knowing her determination she probably would!

'Well?' she barked at Lori's silence.

'Nothing.' Lori stood up to get a gaily-coloured pot from the cupboard under the sink, putting the plant inside and carrying it to the window. 'Smells like chicken,' she teased.

'You looked in the oven,' her aunt dismissed. 'No, not there. Really, Lorraine, do you have no sense? That plant needs more warmth than it will get in that draughty window!'

She moved the plant to one of the shelves in the alcove next to the electric fire, not at all perturbed by her aunt's bluntness, knowing it hid a genuine and constant affection. 'I didn't look in the oven. I know the smell of your cooking a chicken—delicious!'

Only by the slight lessening of her aunt's scowl could she tell she was pleased by the compliment. 'I'm still waiting, Lorraine,' she frowned at her.

Some of her confidence wavered. Aunt Jessie had always been too astute. She should have known she couldn't fool her this time either. 'A friend of mine got married yesterday,' she revealed guardedly.

Her aunt nodded. 'I remember you telling me—You aren't still mooning about that young Judas, are you?' she snapped her displeasure at such an idea.

Lori felt herself blushing. From the moment she had introduced Nigel to her aunt she had known she didn't like him—and the dislike had been mutual. 'A rude, cantakerous old woman,' Nigel had called Aunt Jessie. 'A pompous young know-it-all,' Aunt Jessie had called him. When she had told her aunt of her broken engagement, of the reason for it, Aunt Jessie had assured her she had had a lucky escape. Judas, she called him then, and she still continued to do so.

'No, of course——'

'I know what next week is,' her aunt continued in her brisk no-nonsense voice. 'But whether or not you can accept it, he was never right for you. If he'd really loved you he would have continued to do so even if *you* had been the one accused of stealing.'

Stealing. Her father had never so much as taken a paper-clip from the bank he was manager of! A discrepancy had been found in the accounts during a yearly audit, and as manager her father was chosen as the likeliest candidate to have covered up, and committed, those discrepancies. Despite his strong denials he had been brought to trial. Jacob P. Randell had somehow managed to convince the court that her father was more than just a likely candidate, that he had committed the crime.

'What is it?' Her aunt was watching her with narrowed eyes, getting awkwardly to her feet with the aid of her walking stick, moving easier once she was actually on her feet, discarding the walking stick altogether.

Aunt Jessie was old, despite her efforts to look spritely, and she deserved to live the last of her years in peace. The events of twelve years ago were now a faded nightmare to her. If Lori told her about Luke Randell she would only worry.

'You were right the first time,' she said softly. 'The wedding yesterday upset me.'

'Forget him,' the elderly lady dismissed. 'He isn't worth losing even one night's sleep over. How did the wedding go? Did your friend look nice?'

'Very.' Lori went on to describe the wedding in detail, knowing how her aunt loved to hear about such things. Mrs Jarvis would be told all about it tonight when she came back from spending the day with her married son and his family.

'And who is Jonathan?' her aunt pounced once Lori had told her he had driven her home.

She laughed softly. 'Just a friend, another of the lawyers in the practice.'

'Oh.' Aunt Jessie looked disappointed. 'Do you like him?'

'Yes.'

'Then why isn't he more than just a friend?'

It really was wicked of her to tease her aunt in this way. 'I'm going out with him tomorrow,' she revealed.

'That's better.' Aunt Jessie folded her arms across her chest. She was as tall as Lori, only slightly more rounded, and their family resemblance was obvious. 'You aren't getting any younger, you know.'

'Considering you never married at all . . .' Lori said pointedly. It was an old teasing game of theirs, and one they both enjoyed.

'Not because I didn't have offers,' came her aunt's predictable answer. 'I just didn't want some bossy man running my life for me.'

'Besides, where would he have slept?' Lori said tongue-in-cheek, knowing there was hardly room for the bed in her aunt's bedroom, as the room was full of plants too.

'Cheeky madam!'

'Hungry madam,' she corrected with a laugh. 'When is lunch going to be ready?'

The one sure way to get your life back on an even keel was to spend the day with Aunt Jessie. her no-nonsense view of life brought everything back into perspective, even something like that unexpected meeting with Luke Randell. Maybe it had been inevitable—after all, she had chosen to involve herself in the world of law and lawyers, and that was something in which the Randell family were prominent.

She would accept it for what it was, a chance meeting that should be forgotten by both of them.

Then why did she have a hunted feeling all day Monday, almost as if expecting Luke Randell to suddenly appear in her office? It was a ridiculous feeling, and yet one she couldn't dispel, and she felt a sense of relief when it came to five-thirty and she could go home.

Jonathan came in just as she was putting on her jacket to leave, and held it out for her. 'It's still on for tonight, isn't it?' he seemed anxious.

She put up a hand to release her hair from her collar. Her fingernails were painted the same plum-colour of her lip-gloss, her fingers long and tapered, the skin palely translucent, giving an impression of delicacy, and each movement was one of grace and beauty. 'Did you think it wouldn't be?' she teased, her teeth pearly white as she smiled.

Jonathan's eyes deepened in colour as he looked at her. 'I was hoping it would be.' His voice was husky.

She swung her handbag over her shoulder, checking she had her car keys, and her hair bounced round her face, red-gold in the bright overhead lighting. 'I'm looking forward to it,' she nodded.

He swallowed hard, making her effect on him a little too obvious. 'So am I,' he said eagerly.

'Until later, then,' Lori said briskly.

She had fully expected not to enjoy the evening with Jonathan, but she was pleasantly surprised, liking the quiet restaurant he had picked out, enjoying the meal and wine, *and* the conversation. Jonathan had a wide range of interests she hadn't even guessed at, from hang-gliding to reading a good murder mystery.

'I never get them right,' he admitted with a grin.

'What a confession for a lawyer to make!' she teased, the wine giving her cheeks a healthy glow, her mood having mellowed as the evening progressed.

'Shameful, isn't it?' he nodded.

Lori glanced casually at her wrist-watch. 'I hate to break up the evening . . .' and she really meant it! She had enjoyed herself tonight, the first time in months she had been able to relax like this. 'But it is after eleven, and it's a weekday tomorrow.'

'Mm,' Jonathan nodded, signalling for the bill. 'And we all have to be on our toes tomorrow.'

'We do?' she frowned.

'Of course. I—Thanks,' he said as the waiter left them their bill, glancing at it to place a number of notes on the table. 'Let's go,' he suggested huskily.

Lori was perfectly willing to do that, accepting his help with her jacket before following him outside to the waiting car.

'Why do we have to be on our toes tomorrow?' she

asked with a frown once they were on their way back to her flat.

'Wonder boy has asked to look around the practice.' Jonathan shrugged. 'I suppose after living in America all this time he needs to see how the English do it.'

Lori licked her lips nervously, suddenly knowing exactly who 'Wonder boy' was. 'Luke Randell is coming to the office tomorrow?'

'Yes, he—hey, didn't you know?' Jonathan frowned at her involuntary gasp.

'No.' She swallowed hard, the evening suddenly losing all its enjoyment.

'Mr Hammond mentioned it to me this afternoon. I thought you would know, being his secretary and everything.'

'No.' Her voice was ragged.

'I suppose Mr Hammond must have forgotten to mention it to you.'

'Maybe,' she answered Jonathan woodenly, although she didn't really think that was what had happened at all. Luke Randell was more than capable of asking Claude not to tell her of his visit tomorrow, would enjoy forcing her into a position where she had to be polite to him.

'Did he say when Mr Randell would be arriving?' she asked as casually as she could.

'About ten-thirty,' Jonathan shrugged. 'It's to be an informal visit as far as I could tell.'

'Yes.' She sounded preoccupied, relieved that she had received prior warning of Luke Randell's visit, grateful to Jonathan for that, even though he couldn't possibly realise how much.

The light was on in the flat when Jonathan walked her upstairs, and she knew Sally was already home.

'It's all right,' Jonathan read her plea for understanding. 'It's late anyway. I—Could we do this again some time?'

Lori smiled at his uncertainty, the shadowed hallway throwing into prominence the perfection of her high cheekbones, her eyes warm like honey. 'I'd like that.'

'Really?'

'Yes,' she laughed. 'But not for a few days, hmm? I— I don't usually go out during the week,' she invented, not wanting to get too involved with him. She liked Jonathan, but . . . There was always a but.

'I'll speak to you about it again on Friday,' he accepted eagerly.

'Fine,' she nodded.

'I—Well, I—I'd better be going.' He looked uncomfortable, his gaze seemingly locked on her mouth.

Lori took the initiative and raised her lips to his, wondering how he could appear so confident in court and yet lack the courage to kiss her goodnight.

He didn't lack courage at all, he merely needed a little *en*couragement, and he swept her into his arms to kiss her with a thoroughness that left her breathless.

Lori felt a little dazed as she let herself into the flat, the feeling fading as she saw the telltale cigarette stubs in the ashtray. Dave Greene had been here tonight. Pray God he hadn't decided to share Sally's bed!

But she needn't have worried; her friend and flatmate was alone in her single bed, a smile on her lips. That smile worried Lori, it meant Sally still hadn't discovered what sort of man Dave was. Because when she did she would be far from smiling!

Lori dressed with more than her usual care the next day, conscious of the fact that she would be seeing Luke Randell this morning. She played down her looks, the black suit she wore was not one of her favourites, being too severe in style to be totally flattering, as was the white cotton blouse she wore beneath. The soft cloud of her hair she brushed down severely, and her make-up was almost non-existent. She didn't want to attract the attention of Luke Randell, and the playing down of her beauty was done so subtly it was barely discernible.

At least she thought it was! Claude Hammond's double-take as he came into the office at nine o'clock seemed to say she hadn't been as successful as she thought she had. The cool expression in her steady brown eyes warned him not to make any comment. Wise man that he was, he heeded that warning, softly closing his office door behind him, although he seemed to do it with a puzzled shake of his head.

Ten-twenty-five had Lori going to the kitchen to make Mr Hammond's morning coffee, carefully adding two cups, placing the tray on his desk without a word. As she returned to her own desk in the outer office she schooled her features for the moment Luke Randell walked through the doorway.

At exactly ten-thirty by the Roman-numeralled wooden wall-clock he strode through the doorway. And Lori was glad she had had warning of his arrival! In the grey morning suit at the wedding he had looked devastatingly attractive, now in a navy blue three-piece pin-striped suit he looked breathtaking, oozing self-confidence, and an animal magnetism that he didn't even seem aware of—or if he was he simply accepted it as part of himself.

If he was in the least taken aback by her appearance—or lack of it!—he didn't show it, grinning widely as he breezed over to her desk, looking almost boyish in his pleasure at seeing her again. 'Hello, kitten,' his mouth quirked at the involuntary tightening of her lips. 'I told you we would meet again,' he drawled.

Lori ignored him and pressed the intercom. 'Mr Randell is here to see you, sir,' she informed her employer coolly.

'Show him in, Lori,' Claude's voice boomed. 'Show him in.'

'Now that wasn't nice,' Luke shook his head, leaning against her desk. 'I wanted to talk to you for a few minutes first.'

She stood up and walked to the connecting door. 'Mr Hammond will see you——' somehow Luke Randell had managed to reach the door before she did. For such a big man he moved with amazing grace and speed, blocking her way very effectively as she would have opened the door. 'Would you like to go in?' She remained cool, although his proximity was a little unnerving.

'No,' he told her bluntly, his gaze speculative. 'Have dinner with me tonight.'

'I'm sorry——'

'Why not?' he probed sharply.

Lori sighed, knowing that subtle as it might have been, the severity of her appearance hadn't deterred from her looks at all as far as this man was concerned. 'Because I would rather not,' she refused.

He frowned, his grey eyes thoughtful. 'Why have I made such a bad impression on you?'

'You haven't——'

'Oh yes,' he mused, 'I have.'

'Would you please go in?' Agitation entered her voice now. 'Mr Hammond is expecting you.'

'And I'm here,' he nodded. 'But I'm not quite ready to go in yet.' One hand snaked out and curled about her nape, pulling her slowly towards him. 'I imagine this was for my sake,' he fluffed her hair about her face. 'But don't you know,' he shook his head, his arms encircling her waist as he moulded her body to his, 'that you could be dressed in a sack, and yet to me you would still be the most beautiful thing on two very sexy legs?'

He was like a snake charming a rabbit, and to Lori's fury his strength was such that she couldn't escape him. She moved her head from side to side in an effort to escape the descent of that sensual mouth, knowing she wouldn't be able to bear it if he should kiss her. He had her arms trapped within the circle of his, and her eyes spat her hatred of him as he lowered his head that final couple of inches, claiming her lips with his own.

He kissed like an expert, she could tell that; the movement of his lips on hers was slow and drugging, the tip of his tongue probing the edge of her mouth as her lips stayed firmly clamped together, resisting the intimacy.

His mouth became bolder on hers, his arms tightened, arrogantly assuming that she was putting up only a token resistance.

At last he raised his head. 'Kitten, stop fighting me,' he groaned.

'I'm not——'

'Lori, is—Oh!' A surprised Claude Hammond stood in his open office doorway behind them. 'I couldn't think what was delaying you, Luke. I think I must be older than I realised!' he chuckled in self-derision.

Lori hastily pulled out of Luke's arms and went back to her desk, her face averted. 'I'll have these letters ready directly, Mr Hammond.'

'No hurry,' her employer shrugged. 'For the first time, Luke, I've seen my efficient secretary not so cool. And you're the cause of it!'

Lori noisily fed four fresh sheets of paper into her typewriter, ignoring both men, aware that she was a source of amusement to them.

'See you later, kitten,' Luke drawled as he closed the door behind them.

Her fingers ground down on her typewriter keyboard, all the keys tangling into each other. She put her hands up over her face. Oh, why had she let him get to her in that way!

And the memory of his lips on hers was so overpowering it felt as if he was still kissing her! The feeling was so strong that she had to leave her office to go and thoroughly scrub her face, erasing what little make-up she had been wearing.

Her face was pale in the mirror, her eyes huge and haunted. And haunted was the way she was beginning to feel! So much for Little Miss Cool—she had been made to look like an absolute idiot, and in front of Claude Hammond too! She had made it a policy, since her disastrous engagement to Nigel, of keeping her private life strictly separate from her work, and now in one week she had been out to dinner with one of the seven lawyers in the practice and caught by Mr Hammond kissing a family friend in her office. She *hadn't* been kissing Luke Randell, but to Mr Hammond it must have looked that way.

She determinedly got on with her work once she returned to her desk; the two men were still talking in the inner office.

'Lori, bring in the Danfield file,' Mr Hammond buzzed through to her on the intercom several minutes later.

It was the most important case he was working on at the moment, and she spared a moment to wonder why on earth he should want Luke Randell to see the file. No doubt he had his reasons.

She entered the office after only the briefest of knocks, ignoring the man sitting across from Claude Hammond, although she could feel the way he was looking at her 'sexy legs'. Damn him! He had no right to look at her like that in front of her employer.

Claude Hammond seemed to view her bristling antagonism with amusement, his eyes twinkling up at her as he thanked her. As she turned to leave Luke Randell strolled over and opened the door for her, willing her to look up at him.

Lori refused to raise her gaze above the sensitive hand resting on the door handle. It obviously wasn't the hand of a manual labourer, although it also wasn't the hand of a man who sat behind a desk all day either. There was strength in the supple fingers, sensitivity too.

'I sail,' he murmured.

Now her startled lids were raised, and she looked straight into quizzical grey eyes. 'I beg your pardon?'

'Yes, what do you mean, Luke?' Claude sounded puzzled.

A lazy smile lit the hard features of the other man as he turned to smile at him. 'I was just telling Lori I love to sail.' His gaze returned to her flushed face. 'Perhaps you would like to come with me one day?' he offered softly.

'I get seasick,' she refused in a flat voice, pushing past him.

'I could cure that,' he said gently from behind her, standing between the two offices.

Lori turned as she reached the relative safety of her desk. 'I don't want to be cured.' She looked at him steadily, seeing by the tightening of his cynical mouth that he had caught her double meaning.

'The cure could be worse than the ailment, you mean?' he questioned huskily.

'Undoubtedly.' She gave a distant inclination of her head.

'Have you ever tried it?' His voice dripped with innuendo.

'Several times,' she answered coolly.

'And the—result was always the same?'

'Always.'

He shrugged. 'Perhaps you've just—sailed with the wrong men.'

Her mouth tightened. 'No, I don't think that's it at all, Mr Randell.'

'You don't?' he drawled.

'No,' she said stiffly. 'I just don't think I—like it.'

'Pity,' he murmured dryly. 'It can be so—exhilarating.' He turned back to Claude Hammond. 'You were going to tell me about Danfield,' he was saying as he closed the door behind him.

Lori sank slowly into the chair behind her desk. Lord, why had she let him get her into a conversation like that one! Neither one of them had been talking about sailing, and they both knew it. It had once again been his ability to read her mind that angered her, that had provoked that almost juvenile exchange.

The trouble was that Luke Randell made her *feel* juvenile. Whenever he was around she wanted to snap and snarl at everyone.

CHAPTER FOUR

LUKE was 'around' a lot the next three days, and by the time Friday afternoon arrived Lori was almost at breaking point. It seemed to have become a challenge to the man to get her to go out with him, and his determination to succeed had even prompted her to accept another invitation from Jonathan, when she had had no intention of going out with him again. Luke had made his invitation for Saturday this morning, which as usual she had refused, only to have Jonathan come in a few minutes later and issue another invitation. Remembering the determined glitter in steely grey eyes, she had accepted Jonathan's invitation out of desperation. His unhidden pleasure had made her feel guilty, but at least when Luke had repeated his invitation this afternoon she had been able to say, in all honesty, that she already had a date.

'Anderson?' he had drawled.

'Yes,' she answered with satisfaction.

Luke shook his head. 'He doesn't really mean anything to you.'

Hot colour flooded her cheeks. 'And how would you know that? Don't tell me,' she scorned. 'You know me, right? Only you don't, Mr Randell. And you never will!'

'I won't?'

'No!'

'If I didn't know your aversion to me was genuine, I'd think it was a case of "the lady doth protest too much", but——'

'You *know* my dislike is genuine?' she repeated incredulously.

He was sitting on the side of her desk, one leg swinging idly back and forth. 'Oh yes, I know, kitten,' he was serious now. 'But it makes no difference.'

'To what?'

'My plans to marry you.'

'Oh, for God's sake . . .' She stood up angrily. 'Mr Hammond said you were to go straight into his office once you returned from lunch. I would be grateful if you would do just that.'

He stood slowly to his feet, a good six or seven inches taller than her, even in her high-heeled sandals. 'Anything to make you happy, kitten,' he drawled.

'Anything?'

'Within reason,' he derided her eagerness.

'Stay away from me?'

'Not possible, I'm afraid. Not now, or in the future.'

'Why?' she pleaded.

'You really want an answer to that?' he mocked.

'No,' she sighed.

'Good,' he said with brisk satisfaction. 'I'm wearing you down, bit by bit, aren't I?' With that he went through to join Claude.

Lori wouldn't have believed it was possible for her life to be so upset a second—no, *third* time. First with her father, then with Nigel, and now this hounding by Jacob Randell's son. She had thought after the first half a dozen refusals to his invitations that he would stop asking her and perhaps take out one of the other secretaries who worked here, all of whom would have gone like a shot. But no, it was Lori he was determined to win, and today was far from the first time he had repeated his plans to marry her. It was almost as if to him the whole thing was decided, that he was just trying to break down her final resistance.

He was even at the weekly staff meeting that afternoon, sitting beside Claude Hammond, power in every line of his relaxed body, almost like a sleepy feline. Come to think of it, he looked more like a cat who had stolen a saucer of milk, with a smile of satisfaction playing across his harsh features.

Lori took notes of the casual conversation flowing through the twenty or so people in the room, knowing that Claude would want a typed reminder of what had been discussed. He very often came up with ideas for improving office relations from concentrating on what was said—and sometimes on what *wasn't* said.

Today was a little different. Claude called for silence a few minutes after they had all gathered in the large staff-room.

He stood up. 'Now you may have all noticed Luke Randell in the building for the last week.' There were several ecstatic confirmations by the female members of staff, Lori noticeably not being one of them. 'As from Monday that will become a permanent thing. As you all know, I have been thinking for some time of retiring as an active member of the practice, and Luke has consented to take my place. I'm sure you'll all join with me in——'

Lori didn't listen to any more, didn't take notes either. Luke Randell was coming to *work* here, to take Claude Hammond's place! Where did that, as Claude's secretary, leave her? Certainly not as Luke Randell's secretary!

When it came to the end of the meeting she filed out with everyone else, still deeply shocked. Why hadn't it occurred to her that Claude Hammond was considering taking the other man into the practice; what other reason could he have had for being here? But it hadn't occurred to her, and now the realisation was almost too much to take in.

'That's a turn-up for the books, isn't it?' Jonathan was walking at her side.

'Yes ...' Her voice came out shaky and uncertain, nothing like her usually confident tone.

'I had an idea, of course——'

'You did?' she said almost accusingly.

'Mm,' he nodded, following her into her office. 'And it's a feather in Claude's cap to get such a man for a partner.'

Lori sat down behind her desk. 'I thought, when the time came, that the promotion would come from within.'

Jonathan shook his head. 'It was never suggested. No, I would say Claude has had Randell in mind for some time now. And having spent the last week talking with him, watching him I don't think Claude could have made a better choice. Luke Randell is exactly what this firm needs.'

So much for professional jealousy! It seemed that far from resenting Luke Randell, the younger men were going to admire him.

Well, here was one person who didn't, and who couldn't, and the sooner she handed in her notice the better. She didn't want to leave, far from it, she enjoyed her work here, but she knew she couldn't even stay in the same building as Luke Randell on a permanent basis.

As soon as she got back to her office she typed out her notice, uncaring that everyone would know she had done it because of Luke Randell coming to work here. She had to go away as soon as possible, and by handing in her notice today she could leave in four weeks. Four weeks, when just this one week had dragged by! But it was going to take Claude at least that long to acquaint the new man with all the cases he would be taking over, so that should ease some of the pressure on her.

When the door opened Luke Randell was alone, slowly closing the door behind him, eyeing her almost warily.

'Welcome to Ackroyd, Hammond and Hammond, Mr Randell,' she said stiffly, taking her resignation out of her typewriter and replacing it with an envelope.

His mouth twisted, the light eyes mocking. 'I wish that could have been said with a little more sincerity. Still, we can't have everything, can we?' he added cheerfully.

There was a flush on her cheeks as she typed Mr Hammond's name on the envelope.

'What's this?' Luke Randell had picked up the letter and was reading it even as she made a grab for it.

'That was a private letter,' she told him stiffly.

'It was,' he nodded. 'Although you may as well realise that all mail that comes through this office in future will be read by me. What's the meaning of this?' he tapped her resignation against his leg as he sat on the side of her desk, all teasing gone now, his expression grim.

Her mouth twisted. 'I would have thought that was obvious.'

'Oh, it's obvious,' he nodded. 'It's why that needs explaining.'

Lori looked away. 'I would have thought that was obvious too.'

'Maybe.' His hand was rough on her chin as he wrenched her face round to look at him. 'You're doing this because of me?'

She met his gaze unflinchingly, feeling very uncomfortable with his fingers digging into her flesh. 'Yes,' she snapped.

His mouth compressed into a thin line, the teasing man of the last week completely erased, to be replaced by a man with hard determination, a man who would stop at nothing to get what he wanted. In that moment he looked exactly like his father, and Lori wrenched away from his confining hand, even though it physically hurt her to do so and her skin was red and sore where he had held her.

'You would leave here, a job you obviously enjoy, just because you don't want to work with me?' His voice was deceptively soft as he stood up to look down at her, the charcoal-grey suit accentuating the width of his shoulders, the taut flatness of his stomach, the length of his legs.

'Yes!' her reply came out unhesitatingly.

'You dislike me that much?' he ground out.

'Yes!'

He drew his breath in raggedly, his expression harsh. 'And if I *asked* you not to do it?'

This wasn't the same Luke Randell she had met at Nikki's wedding a week ago, this was Luke Randell the lawyer, and she could see just from this brief glimpse of him that in a courtroom he would be formidable, even more lethal than his father had been at the height of his career.

'It wouldn't make any difference,' she told him distantly. 'I was employed as Mr Hammond's secretary, I prefer to leave if I'll no longer be working for him.'

'I don't think your employment was ever discussed by Claude and myself,' he said coldly. 'I believe Claude had faith in your loyalty to the firm. But if you would prefer to work for Paul I'm sure that could be arranged.'

'Nikki is Paul's secretary.'

'All the more reason for the change. I don't think it's a good idea for a man and wife to work so closely together.'

'*You* don't think?' Lori bristled indignantly on her friends' behalf.

'Maybe you didn't understand the situation clearly, Lori,' he said abruptly. 'Or maybe you weren't listening properly.' His silky tone implied that he had known of her inattentiveness during the meeting, that his shrewd grey eyes had missed none of her withdrawal from the proceedings. 'I am the new *senior* partner. In future we shall be known as Randell, Hammond and Hammond.'

'Paul——'

'Knows all about it,' he said harshly. 'And has done for some time. Although what that has to do with you I have no idea. Unless Paul means more to you than just your friend's husband——'

'How dare you?' Lori gasped her outrage. 'How dare you say such a thing to me?'

'Quite easily, I can assure you,' Luke drawled hardly. 'Although by your reaction I realise I was way off on this one.'

'You certainly were!' She glared at him.

'Yes,' he nodded, 'I can see that. But would you hold back on your resignation for a few months at least?'

'I——'

'Luke, my dear boy,' Claude Hammond came into the room. 'And Lori,' his smile softened apologetically, 'I hope you'll forgive me for my surprise announcement just now, my dear. But I'm sure you'll agree with me that Luke would be an asset to any law firm.'

She could see the derisive twist of Luke Randell's

mouth out of the corner of her eyes, and her resolve to leave deepened. 'I——'

'Maybe Lori doesn't share your opinion, Claude,' Luke drawled.

'I'm quite sure you're an excellent lawyer.' And she was!

'Oh, he is,' Claude confirmed. 'I could hardly believe my luck when he consented to join us.'

'But it—it's so sudden,' she licked her lips nervously. 'I—I thought your retirement wasn't until next year?'

Claude suddenly looked evasive, the smile no longer reaching the warmth of his eyes. 'Luke was able to come to us earlier than expected. And—well, Ruth has been wanting a long holiday for years now. I've decided to take her next week.'

'Next——? But——' she was stopped by a warning look in Luke Randell's eyes, frowning as he gave a barely perceptible shake of his head. Her consternation showed in her face, and he gave yet another shake of his head, more forceful this time, an angry glitter to the grey of his eyes. Lori chewed on her inner lip for several seconds, finally looking up at her employer.

With sudden clarity she saw the strain about Claude's eyes, the hollow greyness of his cheeks, the weight-loss she hadn't been aware of; her thoughts had been occupied with her own problems this last week.

'Where are you going?' she asked with bright interest.

'Oh, we thought a cruise of the Greek islands would be nice,' Claude dismissed casually. 'Now, I just have some last-minute things to see to in my office before I go. Luke?'

'I'll be through in a moment,' he told the other man. 'I'm still trying to persuade Lori into thinking I'm irresistible,' he added lightly.

Claude laughed. 'Good luck, my boy. I have a feeling

you're going to need it!' He gave him a hard slap on the back, still chuckling as he went through to the adjoining office.

Luke Randell's own humour faded the moment he and Lori were alone again. 'Thank you,' he said softly.

Lori sat back in her chair, very pale. 'There is no holiday, is there?' she queried huskily.

'Not for some time, no,' he confirmed.

'Claude isn't well, is he?'

'No,' Luke sighed. 'He has a heart condition——'

'But he's had that for years,' she protested with a frown.

Grey eyes were narrowed on her. 'You knew about it?' he said slowly.

She nodded impatiently. 'I often have to remind him to take his tablets. And he had regular check-ups—He had one two weeks ago,' she realised dully. 'What's wrong with him?' she asked sharply.

'His condition had worsened at the last check-up,' Luke spoke in a blunt, to-the-point voice. 'He needs an operation.'

'And so next week——'

'He's going into hospital.'

'Oh, God!' she groaned in genuine distress. She had become very fond of Claude Hammond since coming to work for him. 'Nikki and Paul . . .' she trailed off.

'Have no idea,' Luke answered her unfinished question. 'If they had they would have cancelled the wedding. And Claude didn't want that. But the operation is vital, so——'

'He sent for you,' Lori said dryly.

'Yes,' Luke bit out, 'he sent for me. And I don't care for your sarcasm. It wasn't exactly convenient for me to pack up my life and return to England at such short notice,' he scowled.

'I'm sorry,' she flushed. 'I can see it can't have been easy for you.'

'I doubt it,' he said dismissively. 'But your understanding isn't that important to me. Claude is, and that includes his peace of mind. I'm here because he wants me here. He and Paul have always been close to me, I couldn't let them down.'

'Just as I can't,' she realised dully, staring into space, looking up at him reluctantly. 'I have to stay on here, don't I.' It was a statement, not a question.

He gave an inclination of his dark head, looking older in his grimness. 'I think so. But of course, the decision lies with you. If you leave now it will upset Claude, but neither I nor anyone else can make you stay.'

She was trapped, he knew she was. Claude was the sort of man who couldn't leave any ends untied. Knowing how he felt about organisation, he was probably already deeply upset about having to leave Luke after only a week. If she turned round, the person who knew almost as much about Claude's cases as he did, and told him she was leaving, he was just as likely to refuse to go in to hospital at all and stay on here himself. She couldn't do that to him.

But neither could she work for Luke Randell! It would be like working with the son of her father's murderer, because Jacob Randell had killed her father as surely as if he had kicked the chair away from beneath his dangling feet.

Some of what she was feeling must have shown in her face. 'As soon as Paul gets back from his honeymoon,' Luke rasped, 'I promise you you can go and work for him. Nikki will probably suit me better anyway.'

The last was said as a deliberate insult, Lori could tell that by the hard glitter of his eyes. And yet she refused to rise to the bait. 'I think that might be for the best,' she gave a distant nod of her head.

'Okay, Lori, if that's the way you want it,' he bit out. 'And let me assure you that in future our own relationship will be purely business.'

She eyed him coolly. 'It's never been anything else as far as I'm concerned.'

'If I had the time . . .' Luke muttered grimly.

'Yes?' she challenged.

He towered over her, the leashed power a tangible thing. 'If I had the time I'd melt that ice right down to your bones,' he told her savagely. 'But in the meantime I'll concentrate on making sure my efficient secretary remains that way.'

'Mr Hammond has never had any complaints,' she said stiffly.

'I'm not Claude,' he derided. 'And I have my own way of doing things.'

'I can assure you my personal dislike of you will not alter my efficiency,' Lori snapped.

'I wish I could be as sure of my desire for you,' he muttered. 'But only time will tell.'

It would indeed. Time when, even though she might hate it, she was going to have to work for this man. She knew the time was going to pass very slowly.

Luke left Claude's office half an hour later, stopping beside her desk. 'I'll see you on Monday morning,' he told her abruptly. 'Nine o'clock sharp.'

'I'll be here,' she said through gritted teeth.

'I'm sure you will,' he scorned. 'The capable Miss Parker!'

Lori ignored the barb, and heard him leave a few seconds later. She was not at all surprised when Claude sent for her, and schooled her features into a casual smile, her pad and pencil in her hand ready for dictation.

'You won't need those, my dear,' he dismissed with a smile. 'Luke told me he's talked to you, so there's no longer any need for pretence between us.'

Her smile instantly faded. 'Oh, Mr Hammond——'

'I know, I know,' he softly accepted her show of distress. 'But I'll be out of hospital before you know it, *then* I'll take Ruth on that holiday. And when I get, back I'll still be involved here in an advisory capacity. I can still show the young ones a thing or two!'

'I'm sure you can.' Lori blinked back the tears at the brave face he was putting on things.

He cleared his throat noisily, showing he wasn't as unaffected as he appeared to be. 'Now what I really wanted to say,' he continued briskly, 'is that I'm pleased you've decided to stay on and work with Luke. He's a fine man, we're lucky to get him.'

'I'm sure you are,' she agreed noncommittally.

'He wasn't actually supposed to have joined us until next year,' Claude spoke almost as if to himself. 'But he very kindly agreed to give up a very lucrative consultancy for an oil firm in the States to come back now. I can't tell you how much that means to me.'

He didn't have to, she could see it in his face. But something puzzled her. 'Why didn't he ever join his father's practice?' It seemed logical that he would have done.

Claude shrugged. 'I don't know the full story, but I do know Luke and his father had a strong clash of personalities—they always have. It was never even a possibility that Luke would go in with his father. Besides, Jacob is retired now.'

If Luke Randell clashed with his father perhaps he wasn't all bad after all! But that didn't change the fact of who he was; that the same cruelty ran through the son as the father.

*

Lori was preoccupied the next evening as she sat across the dinner table from Jonathan, unaware of the admiring glances coming her way, of the male attention her daringly cut black dress was attracting.

But Jonathan was very aware of it, flushed with the pleasure of being the man accompanying the most beautiful woman in the room.

'Is it bothering you that Randell is joining the firm?' he finally asked.

The gold droplet earrings glittered as she swung her head in his direction, the slender necklace about her throat a perfect match in design. They were the only two pieces of jewellery she wore, her fingers were completely without rings, although Jonathan had an idea he was far from the first man to want to be able to put one there.

'I'm sorry?' her voice was husky.

He shrugged. 'I just wondered if you were worried about working for Randell.'

'Didn't I mention that it wouldn't be for long?' She went on to tell him about the change-over with Nikki when she got back from her honeymoon. 'Mr Randell doesn't approve of married couples working so closely together,' she added scathingly.

'Neither do I,' Jonathan told her ruefully, not missing her sarcasm. 'It certainly isn't any way to conduct business, and it can't do the marriage much good either, to be in each other's pockets in that way.'

'Maybe not,' she conceded, although it didn't stop her resenting the fact that Luke Randell felt the same way. 'Don't you think it's a little early to start issuing orders?'

Jonathan shrugged. 'Not if that's the way he feels about it.'

Lori held back her angry retort. Jonathan was

obviously suffering from a severe bout of hero-worship, and for the moment nothing she said would change his opinion of the other man.

She fended off his invitation to go out for the day on Sunday, not wanting to become that involved with him, aware that she had only accepted this second invitation to put Luke Randell off, an act of pure desperation, and not one she was proud of. Jonathan was much too nice a person to be used in that way.

She returned his kiss with only a lukewarm response, reaching up to kiss him on the cheek. 'I had a lovely evening,' she smiled at him. 'Have a nice weekend,' she told him before escaping into the flat, realising from the hollow silence that Sally was once again in bed and asleep before her.

Sally was also up and dressed before her the next morning, and woke Lori with a cup of coffee. 'I'm going out for the day soon, and I thought I'd ask how your date went last night?' She sat cross-legged on the bottom of Lori's bed as she sat up to drink the coffee.

'Fine,' Lori said evasively. 'Are you going out with Dave?' she changed the subject.

'Mm,' her friend nodded.

'Are you serious about each other?' she frowned.

Sally blushed. 'I—I like him—a lot.'

'And Dave?'

Sally shrugged, standing up. 'He likes me too. Come on, I'll cook you breakfast before I go, as I'm feeling generous.'

Lori took the hint that Sally didn't want to discuss Dave any more than she wanted to talk about Jonathan, although she had a feeling it was for different reasons. No matter how many times she met Dave she couldn't quite bring herself to like him, but Sally was an adult, and maybe she knew a different Dave from the one Lori did. Maybe . . .

'Going out with Jonathan today?' The two of them had eaten breakfast, and Sally had come back from the bedroom after dressing for her date.

'Not today.' And never again if she was sensible. Jonathan was the sort of man who would eventually want marriage, the sort of man who could get hurt by her.

'Then I insist you sit down and have another cup of coffee and read the newspaper.' Sally's actions suited her words as she sat Lori down in a chair, putting a cup of coffee in one hand, the newspaper in the other. 'Have to build your strength up for tomorrow with the new boss,' she added teasingly.

'And you have a nice day too!'

Sally laughed at her sarcasm. 'Don't wait up for me.' She sobered, blushing. 'I could be late.'

Lori knew that meant her friend might not be home at all, but she refrained from making any comment, giving a cheerful goodbye as Dave knocked on the door.

It was nice to sit back on the sofa and put her feet up, having been under more of a strain this last week than she realised. At this rate she was likely to be a physical wreck at the end of another three weeks! Her only consolation was that it had proved to be as much of a strain for Luke Randell as it was for her—but for completely different reasons. She could feel him watching her all the time, knew that his desire for her burnt just below the surface. In a way she could feel pleasure in the rejection he must feel at her indifference, and yet in another way she wished they had never met. She had hardly recognised herself this last week, the bitterness, the coldness, and she could feel it once again taking over her life.

At that moment an article in the newspaper caught and held her attention, pain such as she had known only once before ripping through her, and once again tearing her apart.

It was a photograph, of Nigel. And standing next to him, looking ecstatically happy, was his bride! The picture told its own story—Nigel in a grey morning suit, the bride in a white silk dress and flowing veil, both of them looking happy.

Nonetheless, Lori read the short article beneath, and the details of Nigel's marriage the previous day, to Caroline Maughan, an old friend of the family, the daughter of Lord Maughan, knocked all the breath from Lori's body.

Yesterday had been the anniversary of the day her own wedding to Nigel should have taken place, five years ago to the day he should have married *her*!

CHAPTER FIVE

HER first reaction was, how could he? Her second, a little calmer, why shouldn't he?

When they had parted just over five years ago Nigel had made it obvious that he never wanted to see her again, that who she was, who her *father* was, disgusted him. Surely she hadn't been clinging to the dream that he would one day realise he still loved her, that he would return to her like a knight on his charger, sweep her up in his arms and tell her he still loved her? That was romantic nonsense, and could never be reality, not with Nigel.

But she *had* thought that, in the secret recesses of her heart she knew she had; she had lived on that hope for the last five years. Now she had nothing, nothing except an emptiness she would never be able to fill—and a burning anger towards the people who had done this to her. The Randells!

There was no way she could get back at Jacob P. Randell, not now he had retired, but Luke Randell was all too available. And she had the perfect way of getting to him—his own desire for her!

She didn't cry about Nigel's marriage, she had cried herself out five years ago over him. No, anger had once again taken over, and the Randell family, Luke Randell in particular, were going to know all about that anger.

She took one last tormenting look at the photograph of Nigel, at the way his hair still waved slightly, despite being kept styled short, at the warmth of his eyes, his handsome face. He would be thirty-four now, ten years older than her, and yet he remained lean, his morning suit as superbly tailored as his other clothes had always been. He looked as he should have looked on their wedding day, as he would have looked without his father's interference.

The girl at his side looked very young, like an untouched rose fresh with dew. The article said Caroline Maughan was nineteen, and she was described as a redhaired beauty. Redhaired and nineteen, as Lori would have been five years ago. Was it possible that Nigel hadn't been able to forget her either, that he had married someone as much like her as possible? Her heart cried for him if that were the case, as it cried for herself. The Randells had much to answer for—and they *would* answer . . .

None of her resentment showed the next day as she went about her duties as Luke Randell's secretary. And if she leant a little too close as she bent over his desk, or her skirt rode up a little too high as she took dictation, then she gave no sign of noticing it.

But Luke Randell did. He often watched her when he thought she wasn't aware of it, and he was totally aware of her as she moved quietly about the office.

He was out of the office towards late morning, and it was while he was out that Jonathan came to see her. She felt terrible about refusing to go out with him, and had to make it clear to him that she intended to keep refusing him, and the four telephone calls she received for Luke Randell from a husky-voiced American woman did little to improve her mood.

Luke accepted his messages when he came back, making no comment about the repeated telephone calls from the woman called Marilou. As the woman hadn't left a return number Lori could only assume that he knew where to reach her. She hadn't taken into account, when she thought of her plan for revenge, that Luke might have a girl-friend. It could delay things somewhat.

'I'll be out to lunch,' he came through to tell her a few minutes later, very dark and distinguished in a brown three-piece suit, his shirt pale cream.

'Yes, sir,' she accepted coolly.

He stopped by her desk. 'Are you going to lunch yourself?'

She shrugged. 'I would doubt it.' She usually brought a sandwich back to the staff-room.

'No Jonathan today?'

Lori's mouth tightened at the taunt. 'Jonathan isn't my boy-friend. I've only been out with him twice.' She was very aware of her refused lunch invitation with him.

'Since I've been here?'

'Yes.'

His eyes narrowed as he looked into her composed face. 'Protection, Lori?' he said softly.

'Hardly,' she scorned.

He sighed. 'You could give me a little encouragement.'

'Would Marilou like that?' She quirked one mocking brow.

Luke smiled, the harshness of his face instantly dispelled. 'I doubt it, she's a possessive little minx.'

'Then perhaps you shouldn't keep her waiting,' she said waspishly.

He perched on the edge of her desk, the hard length of his thigh pressed up against the carriage of her typewriter so that she couldn't work even if she wanted to. 'Are you going to be one of those secretaries that knows my every move before I know it myself?' he taunted softly.

Lori's head was bent back as she looked at him, her hair soft and silky to her shoulders. 'I thought you were the one who knew my every thought before *I* knew it myself,' she reminded him huskily, moistening her lips with the tip of her tongue, the movement apparently unknowingly provocative.

Luke's eyes narrowed even more. 'I thought I did,' he told her slowly.

'And what do they tell you now?'

He moved forward, his hand clasping her chin between forceful fingers. 'They tell me ... They tell me ...' Icy grey eyes searched enigmatic brown ones, almost gold with a lighter circle around the iris.

'Yes?' she prompted throatily.

He shook his head, sitting back with a smile as he released her. 'They tell me only what you want them to tell me. You've put up a shield, Lori,' he mused.

She masked her irritation. 'Are you sure you haven't just lost your touch?' she taunted.

Luke stood up with a laugh. 'I'll let you know after lunch,' he mocked.

Lori glared after him as he left the office. So she *had* been right about him lunching with the sexy-voiced Marilou. No doubt he would be longer than the usual hour.

About that she was wrong. He returned promptly on the hour, a tiny blonde-haired woman clinging to his arm. Obviously Marilou. And she wasn't as old as she appeared, once looked at closely, possibly in her early twenties at the oldest. First Nigel and now Luke Randell! Didn't men go out with women over twenty-one any more?

Luke made the introductions. 'Marilou decided she had to see the stuffy place I traded in my air-conditioned, super-modern office in the States for,' he explained teasingly.

'It isn't stuffy at all, honey,' the young girl looked appreciatively around the elegance of the light and airy office. 'And Miss Parker isn't at all what I imagined either.' She looked speculatively at Lori.

Luke smiled, obviously enjoying himself. 'Really?' he drawled. 'And just how did you imagine her?' His expression was mocking as he looked at Lori.

'Older,' Marilou said without evasion.

He gave a throaty chuckle of enjoyment. 'And instead she's almost as young as you are. And almost as beautiful.'

Lori saw how Marilou blossomed under this deliberate flattery, her own gaze cool as she looked over at Luke, seeing the mockery in the clear grey depths of his eyes. He was enjoying the younger girl's jealousy—was perhaps hoping to make her a little jealous too? For such a sophisticated man he was being a little obvious. She doubted if he usually entertained women in his office, or that he usually had to go to these lengths to attract a woman.

Luke's eyes narrowed as he seemed aware of the thoughts flickering through her mind, his mouth twisting sardonically. 'Time you were going, minx,' he told Marilou firmly, turning her towards the door. 'Lori and I have a lot of work to do.'

Typical—Marilou had served her purpose, now it was time to send her away like a good little girl! Lori turned away in disgust, picking up some files to begin putting them away. Nevertheless, she was aware of the other couple standing a short distance away.

'Tonight, Luke?' Marilou said throatily, her arms up about his neck. 'Please, honey! I'll be very lonely without you.'

Luke's hands linked loosely at the base of her spine, curving her body into his. 'I could be busy tonight,' he smiled to take the rejection out of his words.

'Working?' she pouted.

'Working,' he nodded.

'With Miss Parker?' The other girl glanced fleetingly at Lori, her eyes hard.

'Possibly,' he returned noncommittally. 'It depends on whether or not I can persuade her to join me.'

'You'll persuade her,' Marilou said throatily. 'I have first-hand knowledge of your persuasive powers.'

'Don't let your father hear you say that!' He moved away from her, pushing the edges of his jacket back to put his hands in his trouser pockets, emphasising the lean flatness of his stomach, the strength of his thighs. 'He could misunderstand it.'

Marilou ran her fingertips over his chest. 'He sent me here to try and persuade you to come back to the States and work for him—any way I can.'

Luke put her firmly away from him. 'I'm sure that didn't include seduction—although I might enjoy it,' he drawled. 'As for going back to the States,' he shot a look at Lori's firmly turned back, 'I'm quite happy where I am.'

Marilou looked at Lori too, her eyes like hard blue pebbles now. 'That's what I'm afraid of,' she snapped.

'We'll talk about this tomorrow, Marilou,' he told her briskly. 'When I take you out to dinner.

Lori moved to sit behind her desk as the other girl kissed Luke lingeringly on the lips, Marilou's jealousy forgotten simply because he had said he would take her out tomorrow. Gullible little fool! Luke could eat up a little girl like this for breakfast and not even know it. Marilou was much too obvious for him, he was a man who would thrive on challenge, would enjoy the chase as much as the capture.

She had deliberately made a study of him this morning, intended knowing him very well before she began her campaign of revenge. Know your enemy, that would be her motto from now on. And Luke Randell was definitely her enemy!

'Goodbye, Miss Parker.' Marilou's smile was triumphant, her hips swaying suggestively as she left, her expensive perfume lingering on in the air.

Lori looked calmly at Luke as he seemed in no hurry to go into his own office. 'Pretty girl,' she remarked conversationally.

'Very,' he nodded.

'Your last employer must value your services very highly to have sent his daughter to—talk to you,' she said mockingly.

Dark brows rose. 'I happen to know Marilou was scheduled for this holiday in England long before I thought about coming back. Gerry may have told Marilou to look me up while she was here, but he certainly wouldn't tell his daughter to do more than that. She's a very—inventive young lady,' he drawled tauntingly.

'I'm sure.' Her mouth twisted, and she looked down at her notebook in dismissal, turning to a new page, her nails kept short for her work, painted with a pale pink gloss.

'And what do you think of my persuasive powers?'

Without her being aware of it he had moved to stand beside her, his breath stirring the hair at her temple, the tangy smell of his aftershave discernible to her senses—deliberately so, she felt. Well, she wasn't affected by his blatant masculinity, and she never would be!

She turned to look at him with cool brown eyes. 'I haven't thought of them—I wasn't aware that you had any,' she added softly.

He straightened, chuckling softly. 'I'll admit that they haven't worked very well with you—yet. But I live in hope.' He took his hands out of his pockets, all humour fading, at once becoming the totally capable lawyer he had been all morning.

Lori hadn't been at all surprised by his efficiency, not after the glowing reports Claude had given him. Neither had she been surprised by the fact that he was familiar with all of Claude's cases. He was that sort of man, he would be proficient at everything he set out to do—even at handling women like Marilou. It appeared Lori was the only weakness he had! And he would be made to pay for that weakness. But not yet; she didn't know him nearly well enough to start her plan yet.

She took her cue from him now, wiping all expression from her face, the competent secretary to his efficiency. 'You have an appointment in ten minutes,' she reminded him crisply. 'And if you really need me to work overtime I am available.'

'No Jonathan?'

'I already told you, no.'

'Just checking.' He shrugged. 'He could have crept in here while I was out at lunch.'

Her eyes flashed, the gold circle around the iris more noticeable, her 'cat's eyes', as Luke called them. 'Jonathan has no need to *creep* anywhere,' she snapped defensively on his behalf.

'Around my office he does,' Luke growled, his grey eyes glacial, his mouth tight.

Lori held back her smile of triumph at this display of jealousy, but her bland expression revealed none of her thoughts. 'We're work colleagues,' her voice was softly self-assured. 'It's only natural that we should talk, swap ideas.'

His face darkened. 'I trust Anderson doesn't tell you about his confidential cases?'

'Of course not!' she flushed indignantly. 'Jonathan is a very responsible lawyer, a very good one.'

Luke's eyes widened. 'You admire him?'

'As a lawyer, yes.'

'I——' he broke off the conversation as the telephone on Lori's desk pealed out. 'Saved by the bell,' he muttered as he went through to the adjoining office.

Lori picked up the receiver, at once engrossed in her work. It was Luke's two-thirty appointment arriving downstairs in reception, and the client was in with him for the next hour. After that it was a race against the clock, Luke needing a confidential report typed and ready for him first thing in the morning.

She was an accurate as well as fast typist, nevertheless it was almost eight o'clock by the time she pulled the last of the finished sheets from her typewriter, placing it on top of the neat pile on her desk.

Luke strolled in from his own office at the silent typewriter, his jacket discarded, his shirt sleeves rolled back, his tie loosened and his shirt collar unbuttoned. He ran a weary hand about his nape, his dark hair slightly ruffled, the grey at his temples looking very distinguished.

He picked up the last of the typewritten sheets, having read the others as she completed them. 'Finished?'

'Yes.' She flexed her aching shoulder muscles, not realising how stiff she had become while engrossed in her work.

'Do you ache?' Luke was watching her intently as she kneaded the nape of her neck tiredly, and his eyes narrowed.

'A little,' she admitted.

He put the typewritten sheet back on her desk and moved round the back of her chair to take over massaging her neck and shoulders. 'Better?' he queried huskily a few seconds later.

She was too busy fighting the urge to push his hands away to appreciate the expert massaging of her taut neck muscles. If she pushed him away she would ruin everything. Playing hard to get was one thing, showing complete aversion was something she would have to fight from now on. His hands touching her now showed her that wouldn't be easy!

'Yes, thank you.' She moved away from him without being too obvious, standing up as if she needed the exercise. 'Are we finished for the day?'

Luke nodded, his eyes narrowed. 'I'll drive you home.'

'I have my own car,' she shook her head.

'Then have dinner with me?' His voice had lowered throatily.

He expected a refusal, she could see by his wearily resigned expression that he did. She would have loved to have accepted, just to see if she could actually make him at a loss for words for once. But it would give her more satisfaction to keep him waiting just a little longer.

'Not tonight,' she refused lightly. 'A hot bath and an early night are what I need right now.'

'I like the sound of that,'

She stiffened at the seduction of his tone. 'So do I,' she deliberately ignored the suggestion in his voice. 'If you'll excuse me . . .'

'Lori!' He stopped her at the door.

Her eyes were cool as she looked at him, at complete variance with the fire of her hair. 'Yes?'

Luke shook his head. 'Never mind,' he dismissed, turning away. 'I'll see you in the morning.'

She drove home as steadily as normal, stopping at all

the red and amber lights, her speed a steady thirty, none of her fevered inner planning shown on the calm complacency of her face.

Luke Randell was a man who used women—he had probably used Marilou to get on in his job with her father's oil company. And he wanted to use her, but for a different reason. He wanted to use her to satisfy a desire he had for her, the offer of marriage the carrot he was dangling in front of her nose. Only he was going to find it took more than the offer to get her into his bed, and that even when their marriage had become a reality he *still* wouldn't have her in his bed.

Her spine tingled with anticipation, anticipation of the day she told Luke Randell who she was, that he was married to the daughter of a supposed criminal, a criminal his father had persecuted until he killed himself. Then she would have her revenge, a revenge more than suited to the crime.

Luke was out of his office the next morning, but Lori had plenty to keep her busy and she was dealing with her filing when he walked in shortly after twelve.

He looked tired, lines fanning out from the corners of his eyes, grooves beside his mouth. He also looked very formal and unapproachable, his black three-piece suit fitting superbly across his wide shoulders and tapered waist, the briefcase he carried of the finest leather.

'Coffee,' he snapped on his way through to his office.

Lori's eyebrows rose as he closed the door decisively behind him. He hadn't spared a glance for the way her bottle-green dress clung to her body, clearly showing the pertness of her breasts, the narrowness of her waist, the slender curve of her thighs. All that had been revealed to him as she stood beside the filing cabinet, and he hadn't even noticed! He couldn't be allowed to get away with such a display of indifference, he had to be almost begging for her by the time she gave in to even her first date with him!

She was smiling brightly when she carried his coffee in to him a few minutes later, sensing his double-take as she placed the steaming cup in front of him.

'You're looking very cheerful,' he scowled, and sat back, his jacket once again disgarded in an attempt to relax after what must have been a tense morning.

The smile remained fixed on her gently curving lips. 'Is there any reason to be miserable?'

'You've heard from the hospital?' tension sharpened his voice.

'Hospital?' she repeated dazedly. 'I—Claude . . .' she realised dully. Dear God, what was the matter with her! Claude was scheduled to have his operation today and she had forgotten all about it. 'I—No,' her voice firmed. 'No one has called. Only the messages I left on your desk.' Several of them, she had noted, were from Marilou.

'You may as well go to lunch now I'm back,' Luke dismissed coldly. 'I can deal with things here.'

Lori left the room with the knowledge that she had gone down in his estimation—and her own. She had been aware of Claude's operation today, of course she had, but the realisation that revenge on the Randells for past wrongs was at last to be hers had pushed it to the back of her mind. Disgust had flashed briefly in Luke's eyes, and she knew he was angry with her.

She was angry with herself! Whatever her private battle with Luke and his father she mustn't let it colour her relationship with other people. Claude and Ruth had been good to her the last two years, Paul too.

She put a call straight through to the hospital once she got back to her desk, only to be told that, 'Mr

Hammond is still in surgery'. Ruth Hammond's sister was still staying over with her from the wedding, and it was she who came on the line to assure Lori that they would call as soon as they had any news.

Lori felt better when she rang off; she knew that she had to get her life back into some sort of order. After all, she couldn't let revenge on Luke Randell take over. Seeing that photograph of Nigel and his bride had knocked her for six, but she had a purpose now, a revenge she intended seeing through to the bitter end.

She had lunch with Sally as usual, in fact this was starting to be the only time she saw her flatmate. The other girl hardly seemed to spend time at the flat now, and she still couldn't dispel her feelings of apprehension for her friend. Not that Sally looked as if she needed worrying about; she was positively glowing, and her conversation was animated as they ate their sandwiches in the staff room.

'What's it like working for the human dynamo?' Sally wanted to know.

'He's very—capable,' she evaded.

'Very handsome too,' Sally grinned. 'Has he asked you out yet?'

'No . . .!'

'Don't look like that,' Sally laughed lightly. 'After the way his eyes were devouring you at the wedding I'd be a fool if I didn't know he fancied you. I was sure he would have asked you out by now.'

'Well . . . Maybe he has,' Lori admitted as she sipped her tea.

'And you turned him down!' Her friend was incredulous. 'How could you refuse someone as gorgeous as him?'

Lori's mouth twisted as she remembered Luke's method of persuasion. No doubt his practised charm and lethal kisses had felled hardier women than her; she just had reason to know she would never find Luke Randell in the least attractive.

'It wasn't difficult,' she replied truthfully.

'You're mad!' Sally groaned.

Lori quirked one brow. 'You're saying that if he asked you out you would accept?'

'Well, no, *I* wouldn't—It's different,' she protested. 'Yes, it is, Lori,' she added at her knowing look. 'I have Dave, but you—Well, you don't have a steady boyfriend,' she finished awkwardly.

'Just how "steady" is Dave?' Lori queried lightly.

Sally blushed. 'He's asked me to move in with him,' she revealed reluctantly.

Lori deliberately kept her face devoid of expression, something she had learnt to do quite easily while her father was on trial, when the press were always eager for any break in her façade of calmness. She had been nicknamed Little Miss Cool in those days, and except for her weakness where Nigel was concerned she had remained that way.

'Yes?' her reply to Sally was noncommittal.

'Do you think I should?' her friend asked in a rush, chewing on her bottom lip, looking very young and vulnerable in that moment.

Lori shrugged. 'It's your decision, and one only you can make. Does Dave want to marry you?'

'Eventually,' Sally blushed again.

'He's not sure?'

'He feels we should live together for a while first,' Sally rushed on to embarrassed speech. 'You know, a sort of trial marriage.'

'I see. And what do you think of that?'

'I—I haven't made my mind up yet,' her friend said vaguely. 'It's a big decision to make.'

Lori longed to tell Sally what she really thought of the idea, longed to tell her that she would be a fool to make such a commitment to Dave when he obviously had no intention of making any sort of commitment himself. But if she told Sally that, and Dave finished with her because of it, then her friend would probably partly blame her. Only Sally could decide what to do about this.

'You're looking pensive,' Luke drawled as she entered the office, sitting on the edge of her desk as if he had been waiting for her return, his jacket back on now.

Lori sat down with unhurried movements. She knew that this time Luke was very much aware of how little she had on under the thin woollen dress. His eyes narrowed appreciatively, a dark smoky grey. 'Which do you prefer?' she said dryly. 'Cheerful or pensive?'

'Actually, neither,' he taunted.

'No?' she met his gaze steadily.

'No,' he smiled, his earlier coldness complete gone. 'I'd prefer to see you willing and aroused in my arms—preferably in my bed too.'

He had wanted to unnerve her, and he had succeeded. There was no way she could stop the blush in her cheeks, although the look she gave him from steady brown eyes had daunted better men. Luke Randell remained unmoved, his eyes warm as he blatantly looked down the vee of her dress at the gentle swell of her breasts. 'I'm afraid that isn't possible,' she told him softly.

'*Afraid*, Lori?' he echoed throatily. 'That's a step forward.'

'Is it?' She forced herself to meet the probe of those steely grey eyes.

His mouth twisted. 'The shield's gone up again, Lori,' he derided.

She knew that, knew that if he could really see what she was thinking he would recoil in shock. She hated his gaze on her, felt as if he touched her with the sensuality burning in his eyes, hated his closeness, and knew he only had to move slightly to actually touch her. And she couldn't bear that, not at the moment.

'What's going on under those lashes?' he taunted her lowered lids, standing up.

Lori breathed an inward sigh of relief at the removal of his physical closeness, and her confidence ebbed slowly back, raising controlled lids. 'Nothing at all, Mr Randell,' her voice was cool. 'What possibly could be?'

He laughed softly, a predatory male who would make any man quake if they came up against him, in any capacity. His method of dealing with women was much more subtle, but he was still the hunter, and the woman would be his captive. This man would always be the aggressor, and she would have to let him think he was in control of their relationship too. But not too much; half of her attraction for him at the moment was her elusiveness.

'I couldn't even hazard a guess,' he shook his head. 'Since that first week I haven't been able to read a single thought.'

She flashed him what she hoped was a mischievous smile, although she had a feeling it looked more triumphant. 'Maybe I have more to hide now?' Her voice was brittle.

'Maybe you do at that,' he mused. 'Well, I'm off to lunch now myself. Oh, and, Lori——' he paused at the door, his hand resting on its handle, a long strong hand, the fingers thin and tapered, unadorned by any rings.

'Yes?' She was instantly tense.

'The hospital called.'

Her expression brightened. It had to be good news,

Luke couldn't possibly have flirted with her as he had done if Claude were in any danger. Claude's wellbeing would also explain Luke's lightning change of mood from before lunch. He was obviously fond of the older man, and had been worried about him.

'He's all right,' she sighed her own relief.

'Yes,' Luke grinned. 'He's going to be in intensive care for a while, but they aren't expecting any complications.'

'Thank God,' she said shakily.

'My sentiments exactly.' Luke sobered. 'I'm going in to see him tomorrow evening, when he's feeling a little less groggy, I don't suppose you would care to come with me?'

Once again he expected a refusal, and she deliberately allowed herself time to think before she turned down this one. She wanted to visit Claude, dearly wanted to see him, and by accepting this invitation she would be raising Luke's hopes that she might accept others.

He could think it anyway!

She nodded her head. 'Yes, I would. Thank you for asking me.'

He might be a supremely self-confident man, a man assured of his own attraction, but her acceptance had completely taken him aback. 'Did you say yes?' he queried softly, disbelievingly.

Her mouth quirked at his stunned expression. 'I did.'

'Dinner afterwards?'

He was pushing his luck, and he knew it. 'I don't think so,' she laughed softly.

Luke sighed. 'I suppose one yes in a day is a breakthrough! Okay, Lori, we'll go and see Claude together tomorrow evening. Mm—together, I think I like the sound of that word when it's applied to you and me. With a little luck—and that persuasion Marilou assures me I have in a lethal amount—we'll be having a lot of togetherness, you and I.' There was a look of promise in his eyes as he left the room.

Togetherness. Yes, they would have a lot of togetherness—and each moment of it would be torture for Luke Randell!

CHAPTER SIX

ONCE again Lori dressed with special care on Wednesday evening, allowing herself the luxury of wearing something really sexy. After all, it was out of working hours.

The pale tan dress, knee-length, was styled like a Japanese kimono, very tight-fitting, defying the severity of the high neck. It was a dress she usually saved for special occasions, but then tonight was in the nature of a special occasion—her first evening with Luke Randell.

Her hair was newly washed, a blazing red cloud, her make-up slightly heavier than usual, emphasising the liquid seduction of her deep brown eyes, the deep plum-coloured lip-gloss adding a moist promise to her lips. High-heeled black sandals showed off the long length of her legs, giving her a height that added to her simple elegance. She looked provocative, but subtly so.

Although she wasn't so sure about the latter when she received Sally's reaction to her appearance; the other girl was having one of her rare evenings at home!

'Goodness!' she gasped as Lori came through from the bedroom, her head bent to attach the gold bangle to her slender wrist, her only piece of jewellery.

Lori looked up at her friend's spontaneous exclaimation. 'Too much?' she grimaced.

Sally considered her appearance for a moment. 'No, I don't think so,' she said slowly. 'If you were just going to visit Mr Hammond, maybe. But as you're going with Luke Randell—no,' she shook her head.

Lori hadn't wanted to look too obvious, had wanted

to attract without appearing to be conscious of it. 'Maybe I should change . . .' she said uncertainly.

'You'll do no such thing,' Sally told her firmly.

'But if the dress is overdone——'

'No dress *could* be overdone with a man like Luke Randell—and if it were I'm sure he would soon have it *un*done,' Sally grinned. 'No, I think you look perfect. You could hardly wear denims and a top to see Mr Hammond——'

'You aren't supposed to know I *am* going to see Mr Hammond,' Lori reminded her, having told Sally about Claude's operation in confidence. 'He's supposed to be on holiday, remember?'

'I've heard it from two other sources today that he's really in hospital,' Sally dismissed. 'You just can't keep things like that quiet. And I think you'll do just perfectly as you are. Mr Hammond could probably do with a bit of cheering up.'

'As long as I don't raise his temperature!'

'There is that,' Sally chuckled.

Luke seemed to approve of her appearance too when he arrived a few minutes later, for his eyes gleamed down at her in open admiration. 'Changed your mind about dinner?' he drawled. 'Or can I eat you here?'

'Come in and be reintroduced to my flatmate,' she said loudly, opening the door wider for him to enter.

'Whoops!' he murmured as he strolled confidently inside.

Lori took a few seconds to take in his own appearance. There was no business suit this evening, instead a pale green high-necked silk shirt, brown fitted trousers, and a brown and green checked sports jacket. There wasn't a hair out of place, the grey at his temples was very distinctive. Yes, he looked very handsome, and Sally was already scrambling to her feet, looking selfconscious in her casual denims and tee-shirt.

'The other bridesmaid,' Luke smiled, shaking her hand warmly. 'And Kenneth Mitchell's secretary.'

'That's right!' Sally gave a delighted laugh at his knowing her.

He glanced round at Lori. 'I had no idea the two of you shared a flat.'—

'For a couple of years now,' Sally supplied, obviously enjoying talking to him.

Lori watched as Luke charmed the other girl for several more minutes, a contemptuous twist to her mouth, although the emotion was quickly masked as Luke turned to her and suggested it was time to leave.

She wasn't in the least surprised by the car he drove, a silver Jaguar, the sporty model; the atmosphere in the confined front of the car was very intimate.

'Nice girl,' he remarked on the drive to the hospital.

'Yes.'

'Still seeing the man she was with at the wedding?' he frowned.

Her eyes widened in surprise. 'Yes.'

'Hm,' he looked thoughtful. 'Is he always that— neglectful of her?'

Heavens, he was perceptive, more so than she had realised! She would have to be careful tonight, more careful than she had planned on being. Dave *was* neglectful of Sally, unless he wanted something, and this man had known that just through that one meeting with him.

'I have no idea.' She wasn't going to discuss Sally's personal business with him. He was, after all, the new boss.

'You do,' he drawled. 'But you think I should mind

my own business. I liked her,' he shrugged. 'I wouldn't like to see her get hurt.'

'She's a big girl,' Lori told him stiffly. 'And big girls have to make their own mistakes.'

'As you did?' he questioned softly.

Her breath caught in her throat. 'Sorry?' she managed in a casual voice.

'Well, as you seem to have plenty of friends, and you get on well with older people such as Ruth and Claude, I have to assume it's only men you're wary of, relatively young men. Is that it, Lori?' His voice gentled. 'Did you get hurt in the past?'

'You forget, I have Jonathan,' she said woodenly, again knowing the extent of his perception.

'I have it from your own lips that he isn't a boy-friend.'

Her eyes glittered. 'He's a male friend.'

'Not the same thing at all,' Luke derided. 'When was the last time you had a boy-friend, one who kissed you goodnight and who you didn't want to stop?'

'Mind your own damned business!' she snapped.

'Did you ever have a boy-friend like that?'

'Of course I did!'

'When?'

Lori drew in a steadying breath, realising he had her on the run. She wouldn't let him unnerve her, although she had never met anyone who spoke as bluntly as this man. He wanted her, he told her so, and he wanted to know about the other men in her life, so he asked her about them. Blunt to the point of rudeness! Even if her interest in him had been genuine she wouldn't ask him such personal questions. Not that she really needed to; this man oozed experience, a confidence in his power over women.

'I was engaged once,' she revealed coldly.

His interest quickened, a dark frown to his brow. 'Why didn't you marry him?'

'Because I changed my mind,' she lied. 'It's a woman's prerogative, you know.'

Luke turned the car into the hospital gates, slowing it down drastically as he drove through the neat and pretty grounds to Claude's ward. 'I wouldn't have let you change your mind,' he told her grimly as he backed the car into a parking space, looking directly at her once he had turned off the ignition. 'How long ago was this?' His eyes were narrowed, his arm along the back of her seat, his aftershave smelling faintly herbal, his male warmth reaching out to her. His fingers moved to idly play with the hair at her nape, caressing the silky curls. 'How long, Lori?' he prompted hardly.

She shrugged, bending forward to retrieve her handbag from the floor, effectively moving away from his touch without being too obvious. Nevertheless, she saw anger flare briefly in the icy grey eyes. 'A couple of years,' she replied lightly, and opened her car door, the slit up the side of her dress giving him a momentary glimpse of her silky thighs as she swung out of the car, something she seemed unaware of as she turned back to look at him. 'Shouldn't we be going in now? Visiting time is limited, isn't it?'

He got out to join her, locking the doors by the central locking system on his door. 'For the moment,' he nodded. 'Although Ruth's been with him most of the time.' He held her elbow as they followed the signs to Claude's ward, their footsteps echoing eerily in the deserted corridor. 'How many years, Lori?' he persisted softly.

She couldn't hold back her start of surprise. She had thought the subject of her engagement forgotten—she should have realised that Luke's razor-sharp mind wouldn't accept such an evasive reply. 'Four or five,' she dismissed easily. 'I really can't remember.'

He looked down at her, his mouth grim. 'Can't you?'

'No.'

'You didn't love him, then?' he bit out.

She was perfectly in control now, her cool expression gave nothing away. 'I suppose at the time I must have done.'

'You can't remember that either, hmm?' he quirked a derisive brow. 'What a shocking memory you have, Lori!'

'Isn't it?' she said sweetly, pushing open the door to the room Claude had been moved to only that morning. At once all antagonism left her. Claude looked so different from when she had last seen him, his skin drawn tautly across his cheeks, and he was very pale, although the smile he directed at them was familiar enough.

'My dear!' he held out a hand to Lori, the warmth deepening in his eyes as she went to his side.

'And Luke!' Ruth stood up, bearing the strain of the last few days with only the increased lines about her eyes visible, her smile as warm as her husband's in her relief that the danger was at last over.

Luke kissed the other woman on the cheek, bending down to shake Claude's hand, more gentleness in his face than Lori had ever thought to see. 'We won't stay long,' he said softly. 'Just long enough to assure you that Lori and I are getting along just fine. And that she hasn't thrown anything at me yet!' He straightened with a mocking smile in her direction.

She ignored that smile. 'Which isn't to say I won't,' she told Claude sweetly.

The older man chuckled, although even that small effort seemed to tire him, Lori noticed. 'I think you've both more than met your match,' he mused.

'You could be right,' Luke drawled, pulling up a chair for Lori.

She slid into it gracefully, seemingly unaware of the way his hand rested possessively on the back of the chair, also choosing to ignore his slightly intimate way of talking to and about her. If he believed he was making progress all the better, his disappointment would be all the more acute later on when she said a polite goodnight to him!

When they said goodbye to Ruth and Claude half an hour later she allowed him to put his arm casually about her waist to guide her out of the room. But she made sure she moved pointedly out of the arc of that arm once they were out in the corridor, staring straight ahead as she sensed his frustrated gaze on her.

He held the door open for her to get into the car, going round to slide in behind the wheel. 'Dinner?'

'I've already eaten,' she refused, drawing attention to her legs as she smoothed the silky material over her thighs.

'I haven't,' he said curtly.

Lori shrugged. 'Then you can go on somewhere after you've dropped me off at my home.'

'I'd rather you came with me.'

'I have some washing to do this evening.'

'Ouch!' Luke grimaced. 'Second to a lot of dirty washing!'

He wasn't even second! 'Actually,' she looked at him with cool eyes, 'if I weren't doing my washing I still have some ironing to do, or the flat to clean, or——'

'Okay, Lori,' he rasped, 'I get the message.'

She held back her smile of satisfaction with an effort. Luke obviously didn't appreciate this blow to his ego. She felt sure Marilou would have cancelled anything to spend the evening with Luke Randell.

'Don't you ever eat at home?' she asked curiously. 'Or didn't you and Marilou eat out last night?'

'I do eat at home, and yes, Marilou and I did go out last night. But if you're offering to cook me dinner——'

'I'm not,' she told him sharply.

'I thought not,' he drawled with a sigh. 'But if you ever do get the urge to try your culinary skills on someone, I'm always available.'

Lori raised her eyebrows. 'How would Marilou feel about that?' she taunted.

'She can't cook,' he shrugged.

'What a shame! But I'm sure she has other— attributes.'

'I wouldn't know.' His tone was abrupt. 'She only arrived back from the expensive school Gerry sent her to a month before I left the States, and I don't make a habit of seducing children. Good God, Lori, I'm thirty-nine. Marilou is only twenty!'

'So?'

'So I don't make love to adolescents,' he ground out as he stopped the car outside the building containing her flat. 'But I have no objection to melting icebergs!' He pulled her roughly into his arms, grinding his mouth down savagely on hers, at the end of his endurance where she was concerned.

She didn't fight him, but she didn't respond either, forcing herself to remain passive as his mouth raped hers, searching the warm recesses of her mouth, caring nothing for the fact that she wasn't kissing him back.

'Kitten!' he groaned against her throat. 'Don't be cold, darling. Kiss me back!'

Lori almost flinched at his use of the endearment, hating the soft darkness of his hair against her cheek the feel of his lips probing her throat. When his mouth

Say Hello to Yesterday
Holly Weston had done it all alone.

She had raised her small son and worked her way up to features writer for a major newspaper. Still the bitterness of the the past seven years lingered.

She had been very young when she married Nick Falconer—but old enough to lose her heart completely when he left. Despite her success in her new life, her old one haunted her.

But it was over and done with—until an assignment in Greece brought her face to face with Nick, and all she was trying to forget. . . .

Time of the Temptress
The game must be played his way!

Rebellion against a cushioned, controlled life had landed Eve Tarrant in Africa. Now only the tough mercenary Wade O'Mara stood between her and possible death in the wild, revolution-torn jungle.

But the real danger was Wade himself—he had made Eve aware of herself as a woman.

"I saved your neck, so you feel you owe me something," Wade said. "But you don't owe me a thing, Eve. Get away from me." She knew she could make him lose his head if she tried. But that wouldn't solve anything. . . .

Your Romantic Adventure Starts Here.

Born Out of Love
It had to be coincidence!

Charlotte stared at the man through a mist of confusion. It was Logan. An older Logan, of course, but unmistakably the man who had ravaged her emotions and then abandoned her all those years ago.

She ought to feel angry. She ought to feel resentful and cheated. Instead, she was apprehensive—terrified at the complications he could create.

"We are not through, Charlotte," he told her flatly. "I sometimes think we haven't even begun."

Man's World
Kate was finished with love for good.

Kate's new boss, features editor Eliot Holman, might have devastating charms—but Kate couldn't care less, even if it was obvious that he was interested in her.

Everyone, including Eliot, thought Kate was grieving over the loss of her husband, Toby. She kept it a carefully guarded secret just how cruelly Toby had treated her and how terrified she was of trusting men again.

But Eliot refused to leave her alone, which only served to infuriate her. He was no different from any other man. . . or was he?

These FOUR free Harlequin Presents novels allow you to enter the world of romance, love and desire. As a member of the Harlequin Home Subscription Plan, you can continue to experience all the moods of love. You'll be inspired by moments so real...so moving...you won't want them to end. So start your own Harlequin Presents adventure by returning the reply card below. <u>DO IT TODAY!</u>

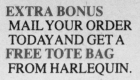

EXTRA BONUS
MAIL YOUR ORDER
TODAY AND GET A
FREE TOTE BAG
FROM HARLEQUIN.

Business Reply Mail
No Postage Stamp Necessary
if Mailed in Canada

Postage will be paid by

Harlequin Reader Service
649 Ontario Street
Stratford, Ontario
N5A 9Z9

Canada Post
Postes Canada
021

returned to hers she knew she couldn't stand it any longer; a vivid picture of her father and Jacob Randell on the front page of a newspaper sprang to mind, this man's father triumphant, her own father the accused.

'No!' she wrenched away from him, looking up at him with tear-filled eyes.

'Kitten——'

'Stop it——' she pushed open the door. 'Stop it, I tell you! My name is Lori, and I am not your kitten! Neither does my ice need melting—not by you, anyway!'

'Lori, I'm sorry,' he grasped her arm, his fingers painful on her bare arm, 'I didn't mean to upset you.' Puzzlement flickered in and out of his eyes. 'Why *are* you so upset? I'm sure you've been kissed before.' He frowned darkly, his face flushed with a deep anger that she should react to him like this.

She chewed on her inner lip, realising she hadn't handled this very well. She should have cooly rejected his kiss, not reacted like some gauche schoolgirl who had never been kissed.

'Yes, I—Of course I've been kissed before,' she attempted to smile. 'But not in anger.'

'I'm sorry,' he touched her cheek with gentle fingertips. 'You had every reason to suppose what you did about Marilou, but I can assure you, if you're interested,' he added ruefully, 'that she is just my ex-employer's daughter as far as I'm concerned. She goes back to the States at the weekend, and all I'll feel is relief. Have dinner with me tomorrow, Lori?' he pleaded softly.

She hesitated deliberately, and saw triumph flare in the depths of his eyes. He thought he had won! He really thought an apology, an explanation that Marilou was no serious competition to her, and a few caresses would have her eating out of his hand. Arrogant fool. As arrogant as his father!

'I don't think so,' she refused hardly, getting out of the car, turning to add, 'I'll be doing my ironing tomorrow.' She slammed the door, making no haste as she entered the building, knowing Luke would be too angry to attempt to follow her. She was right; the soft purr of the Jaguar's powerful engine roared to life as he accelerated away.

A smile curved her lips as she took the lift up to her flat.

To say Luke was brusque with her the next two days would be an understatement—he was positively ruthless.

So much so that Lori began to wonder if she might not have pushed him just too far. He barely looked at her now, and she might have been part of the furniture for all the notice he took of the flattering dresses she wore. And the perfume that the extravagantly decorated box assured her would have a sensual effect on men did the opposite to Luke.

'What the hell is that smell?' he growled as he came into the office on Friday morning, his expression grim. 'For God's sake, open a window!' He slammed into the adjoining room.

She did as he instructed, she also went to the ladies' room down the corridor and washed the perfume from her skin. So much for that!

His humour hadn't improved as he gave dictation, and she felt as if she had been through a battle by the time she returned to her own office—and lost it! Maybe she had gone just a little too far with that last parting comment on Wednesday night, it would certainly seem so. She would have to think of some way to persuade him that she was available—to a certain extent.

He walked out lunchtime without a word, giving her no chance to persuade him of anything. Consequently she was in no mood to cope with Marilou's straightforward talking when the girl walked in five minutes later, her perfume stronger than the one Lori had more or less been ordered to wash off, and the dress she had on leaving nothing to the imagination.

'Luke—Mr Randell has already gone to lunch,' she told the young girl distantly.

Marilou's gaze flickered over her insolently. 'What a pity,' she drawled confidently. 'I thought I was early.' She glanced at her wrist-watch. 'Oh well, I'll have to meet him at the restaurant as we arranged.'

Lori nodded. 'Goodbye, Miss—I hope you have a pleasant flight home tomorrow.'

'Flight?' Hard blue eyes looked at her. 'But I'm not going home.' Marilou shook her head.

Lori met her gaze steadily. 'Mr Randell told me you were leaving tomorrow.'

Marilou smiled, a smile that didn't quite reach her eyes, not even attempting to hide her dislike of Lori. 'I've changed my mind—or rather, Luke changed it for me. Although I haven't told him yet, it's my little surprise for him,' she added with satisfaction.

'I'm sure he'll be pleased,' she said stiltedly.

'So am I,' Marilou smiled like a satisfied cat. 'It was nice seeing you again, Lori,' she said insolently, and left as suddenly as she had entered.

Lori realised that she had no more time to lose; Luke couldn't be as uninterested in Marilou as he claimed if he were still seeing her, if he had asked her to delay her departure. She would have to change her own tactics, she couldn't let Marilou get too much of a foothold in Luke's life. That little madam would cling like a leech, given the chance. Lori couldn't give her that chance; she didn't intend this farce to go on with Luke any longer than it had to.

He appeared to be in a better mood when he came back from lunch—and she didn't need two guesses why!

She rose from her desk to collect her jacket, moving close to Luke, appearing to slip, breathing her satisfaction as she felt his arms go about her protectively.

'Steady,' he murmured close to her ear. 'It's those damned high heels you women insist on wearing.' He put her firmly away from him. Lori at once winced, and Luke's face darkened with concern. 'Did you hurt yourself?'

'Just my ankle.' Her voice was husky, knowing his gaze followed her as she massaged the silky flesh. 'I——' she straightened, meeting his gaze, and her own eyes filled with a forced longing, her lips parting invitingly.

Desire flared in the dark grey depths, and he took an involuntary step towards her, only to stop hesitantly. 'Can you walk all right?' he queried softly, visibly shaken by her closeness.

'I think so.' Her tone was breathless. 'Please don't concern yourself with me,' she dismissed. 'I'm sure you have lots of work you should be doing.'

'Don't be ridiculous,' he was frowning heavily. 'Maybe you should put a cold bandage on your ankle, in case it swells.'

'Oh, I'm sure it isn't that serious,' she assured him hastily, taking several steps with only the slightest of limps. 'I'll be fine in a few minutes.'

His gaze seemed fixed on the perfection of her long legs, the skin soft and silky, tanned from several afternoons spent in the sun. 'Did you know you have the most incredibly sexy legs?' he said huskily.

Warm pleasure filled her. It was working, already it

was working! 'I believe you have mentioned it before,' she looked at him beneath lowered lashes.

Luke groaned low in his throat. 'When are you going to put me out of my misery and go out to dinner with me?' His eyes glittered like black coals, his hands moving restlessly at his sides, as if he would like to touch her.

'How about tonight?' she smiled.

'You mean it?' he took her in his arms.

'Yes,' Lori nodded. 'Unless you have a previous engagement? With Marilou, for example.'

Luke moulded her against the hardness of his body. 'If I had I'd break it. You see, my family's word isn't its bond,' he teased huskily.

She knew he was flirting with her, that he was just trying to make her laugh, and yet his mockery of the claim she had once made to him only succeeded in hardening her resolve to break this man, as her father had been broken.

The door suddenly opened behind them. 'Lori, I——' Jonathan came to an abrupt halt in the doorway, his mouth falling open in surprise as he saw Lori was in Luke Randell's arms. 'Excuse me,' he mumbled, quickly leaving again.

It wasn't the way she had wanted Jonathan to find out about herself and Luke, although his invitations had been increasingly difficult to turn down without being rude. She doubted he would make any more!

Luke watched the display of emotions across her face, her regret, her dismay, and finally her acceptance. 'Like me to go after him and explain?' he said huskily.

She looked up at him with clear brown eyes. 'Explain what?'

'Well, that we—that I——' he frowned. 'Hm, explain what?' he shrugged dismissively. 'He really was just a friend as far as you were concerned, wasn't he, Lori?'

'Yes.' Her arms were up about his neck, clasped together at his nape.

'I never, ever, settle for friendship,' he warned before his lips claimed hers in a kiss of exploration, no force this time, no demand, just very gentle persuasion.

Her lips moved in response beneath his, tentatively at first, and then with an eagerness that had her pulling away from him in surprise. This was an act, she wasn't supposed to *enjoy* it. Not with Luke *Randell!*

'Kitten?' Luke touched her pale cheeks. 'It isn't your ankle, is it?'

'No,' her smile was bright. 'What time will you call for me tonight?'

When she returned from lunch, her ankle suitably cured, Luke's mood had softened towards her; his attraction to her was once more a tangible thing, the warm looks he kept shooting her, and the feeble excuses he used to come into her office making her tease him about the whole practice realising they were going out together. His answer was, 'To hell with what everyone else thinks!'

Luke was still working when she left shortly after five, but he assured her that he would pick her up promptly at eight o'clock. To her dismay she met Jonathan out in the car park, his expression reproachful.

'I'm sorry, Jonathan,' she sighed, not knowing what else to say. She had only been out with him twice, had refused his other invitations, but nevertheless she still felt guilty about him having seen her with Luke.

'So am I,' he muttered. 'I thought you liked me, Lori.'

'I do like you.'

'But you like Randell more.' He grimaced. 'I suppose a senior partner does have more to offer than a mere lawyer.'

She must have hurt him more than she realised, bitterness wasn't usually part of Jonathan's nature. She put her hand on his arm, and felt him tense beneath her fingertips. 'I really am sorry, Jonathan,' she said with a sincerity he couldn't possibly doubt. 'I never meant to hurt you, I only wanted us to be friends.'

'You knew I wanted more than that.'

'Yes,' she confirmed huskily. 'Which is why I haven't been out with you again,' she pointed out gently.

He still looked disappointed, but less angry. 'You're serious about Randell, then?'

'I—I could be,' she answered evasively.

He sighed. 'Then it only remains for me to wish you luck. I wish things could have turned out differently,' he shrugged, 'but Randell's pretty stiff competition.'

'Oh, Jonathan!' Lori spluttered with laughter as she saw his rueful grin.

'Well, he is,' he returned her smile. 'I hope you'll be happy with him,' he bent and kissed her lightly on the lips, 'but if it doesn't work out, I'm still available.'

Lori shook her head. 'I couldn't do that to you. But thank you.'

She felt slightly better as she drove home. She did not like hurting Jonathan, but she knew she couldn't have the complication of him in her life while she was seeing Luke. She doubted he was the sort of man who liked to share anything, especially a woman.

She had proof of that earlier than she had imagined. Luke arrived at her flat at seven-thirty, his expression grim as he walked past her and into the lounge, seeming unaware of the fact that she was still only wearing the robe she had slipped on after her shower. Her hair had already dried, to a glowing red-gold cloud, her make-up was completed too, so she only had her dress to put on.

She followed Luke slowly, frowning at the aggression

in his face, very much aware that they were alone in the flat, as Sally had already gone out. Luke stood with his back to the window, his black dinner suit fitting him superbly, his silk shirt snowy white, emphasising the tanned mahogany of his skin.

'I thought you said eight o'clock,' she frowned, sure that she hadn't made a mistake about that.

'I did,' he bit out.

She moistened her lips, her eyes a puzzled golden brown. 'Then you're early. As you can see, I'm not ready yet——'

'Is he here?' Luke rasped.

'He?' she repeated softly, having no idea what he was talking about.

'Anderson,' he said savagely. 'Is he here? Is that why you're dressed like that, because you've just got out of bed with him?'

She gasped. 'Certainly not! I've just taken a shower, that's why I'm dressed like this. Why on earth should Jonathan be here?' She was genuinely suprised that he should think such a thing.

'My office looks over the car park, Lori,' he ground out. 'I saw you and him there together tonight, the touching little way you put your hand on his arm, the way he *kissed* you,' the last came out fiercely. 'Especially the way he kissed you!'

He was jealous, she could see that now. Luke Randell was fiercely, savagely jealous! She could hardly believe he would react so violently; anger was twisting his face into a cruel mask. Usually he was so controlled, lazily mocking when angry, teasing when he was flirtatious. But he wasn't teasing now, and he certainly wasn't lazily mocking either!

'Luke——'

'Don't try and make excuses, Lori!' he pulled her

roughly towards him. 'It will take more than excuses to placate me, to put the memory of him kissing you from my mind!'

She looked up at him fearlessly, still tall even in her bare feet. 'What will it take, Luke?' she murmured softly, lowering her lashes over honey-coloured eyes, tempting him into action.

'This!' His mouth came down on hers, plundering her mouth, gently easing it apart to run the tip of his tongue along the softness of her lips. 'Kitten!' he groaned, enfolding her in his arms, his hands strong and sure across her back as he moulded her against him, making her aware of the aroused hardness of his body.

To her surprise she felt no revulsion at the intimacy, offering no resistance as he parted the lapels of her robe, one hand moving inside to cup her breast, his thumbtip finding the nipple with unerring accuracy.

Lori gasped and would have moved away, but Luke's arms tightened about her. And then she didn't want to move away, but melted against him, telling herself that she had to allow him to kiss her, to touch her, otherwise he would never desire her to the extent she wanted him to, where he would grant her least little wish to please her.

His lips left hers to travel down her throat to her breasts, capturing one erect nipple between his teeth and lips, running his tongue caressingly along the tip, evoking pleasure with every brushing stroke.

Lori clutched on to his shoulders for support as her knees threatened to buckle and no longer hold her. She had to stop this, and stop it now. Allowing him to kiss her was one thing, to caress her a little too, but if she didn't stop him now Luke would want more than kisses and caresses; he was even now touching her inner thigh, making an exploratory journey to the heart of her sexuality.

She pulled back with a breathless laugh, knowing by the dark glaze of his eyes that he was having difficulty regaining his control; his mouth was very sensual, the desire burning in his eyes.

He straightened with an effort, his dark hair ruffled from where her fingers had clasped on to him in the peak of her sexual excitement. 'Sorry, kitten,' he said raggedly. 'It was just—Seeing Anderson touching you filled me with a black rage, a rage I've had two hours to ponder,' he added ruefully. 'I didn't mean to hurt you. Forgive me?'

She could see he was still unsure of her, had no idea what her reaction was going to be to his anger, to the onslaught of desire that had followed. And off balance was the way she wanted him to remain. If he should ever feel sure of her she would lose her power over him.

'I'll go and finish dressing,' she told him in a brittle voice, giving him no reaction at all. 'Make yourself comfortable,' she invited. 'I shouldn't be long.'

He began to say something and then stopped, sitting down to watch her as she went through to her bedroom, closing the door firmly behind her.

She leant back against it, allowing the weakness she daren't show in front of him, to wash over her, her legs still trembling. Her tentative enjoyment of his touch this afternoon had turned to a blazing fire, a fire she had had trouble putting out—although she had a feeling it had only been dampened down.

Being attracted to Luke—in a purely physical way— wasn't something she had even considered when she had thought of this plan for revenge, sure that she would be immune to the attractions of Jacob Randell's son.

It was a definite complication, but not one she couldn't handle. Luke might be a passionate man, deeply so, but he wasn't a savage, and if at any time she said no to their lovemaking he would respect that.

The possibility that she might one day not want to say no didn't occur to her . . .

Dinner was a lighthearted affair, with Luke seeming determined to charm her, making no reference to their lovemaking earlier, just seeming satisfied within himself that it had happened.

The restaurant was one of the most exclusive—and expensive—in London, the service quietly efficient, and Lori's wine glass was kept constantly filled by the unobtrusive wine-waiter. Luke was obviously accustomed to such service, accepting it with an arrogance that only seemed to make the staff more attentive.

But Luke had eyes only for her, his gaze often resting heatedly on the gentle swell of her breasts as they pressed against the softness of her black fitted gown. Her lips curved in satisfaction as she often caught and held that gaze. Much as he tried to hide it Luke was still deeply affected by their time together in her flat, and when her hand touched his as if by accident as it lay on the table she felt his fingers tremble slightly before his fingers turned to capture hers, the thumb gently caressing as they talked.

He was a good conversationalist, with a knowledge of many subjects, from the theatre to politics, both here and in other countries, to a deep and varied interest in books.

For most of the evening Lori had no need to pretend enjoyment, finding she and Luke had a lot of similar interests, and where they didn't agree they were able to argue lightly. That was, until Luke asked about her family, and then all the enjoyment went out of the evening for her as she remembered who this man was, no longer seeing him as the interesting companion of the evening but as the son of the man who had started the ruination of her life, who had taken everyone from her that she loved, her father, her mother, Nigel . . .

'I don't have any family now,' she told him sharply, removing her hand from his. 'Only my father's aunt. She's in an old people's home—at her own request,' she added defensively, knowing the cruel assumption a lot of people made about such things. And Aunt Jessie would never have gone anywhere she didn't want to! 'I'm very fond of her.'

'I can see that,' he frowned. 'Lori——'

'And how about you?' she questioned brightly. 'What family do you have?'

'Just my father,' his voice cooled too. 'My mother died several years ago.'

'I'm sorry. Your father is Jacob Randell, isn't he?' she asked with a casualness she was far from feeling.

'Yes,' he grimaced.

'But he's famous!'

'Yes.'

'Luke——'

'Can we get out of here?' he rasped, smiling to take the sting out of his words. 'I want to be alone with you,' he added throatily.

The last was meant as a balm against his sharpness, but it didn't erase her curiosity. Claude had told her that Luke and his father had a clash of personalities, could it possibly be that Luke resented his father's fame? Not that she thought him a man with jealousy over his career, he was too accomplished himself for that, but as Jonathan had pointed out after Nikki and

Paul's wedding, Jacob Randell must be hard to live up to.

They drove home in silence, although not a tense one, the sound of the latest Barry Manilow tape filled the car.

'I went to see his last concert at the Albert Hall,' Lori told Luke softly.

'Did you like it?'

'Fantastic,' she answered without hesitation. 'Have you ever seen him in concert?'

'Once,' he nodded. 'I enjoyed it too.'

This was an aspect of music that they hadn't discussed earlier in the evening, and it surprised Lori that Luke should like Barry Manilow. Not that he wasn't an extremely good singer, was a superstar, but he sang mostly romantic songs. Luke didn't come over as a romantic person—sensual, but not romantic.

'I also like your perfume,' he added ruefully. 'Which I was very rude about this morning.'

'You knew——'

'Yes,' he smiled at her indignant gasp. 'It's you exactly. Fiery, with a latent hint of sensuality.' He laughed softly as she blushed. 'I think that's why I got so damned angry, it reminded me too much that all that fire and excitement was out of my reach.' His hand moved to touch her thigh. 'At least, I thought it was,' he added suggestively.

'Did you like your surprise from Marilou at lunchtime?' she diverted his attention from her, seeing him frown as his hand returned to the steering-wheel. He had kissed and touched her enough for one day!

'What surprise?'

'That she isn't going back to America.'

'She isn't?' he frowned darkly, as he stopped the Jaguar in front of her home.

'She said not.' Now it was Lori's turn to look puzzled. 'She came to meet you for lunch at the office, but as you'd already left for the restaurant she missed you. I presumed she would have told you when you met later. I'm sorry if I've ruined her surprise.'

'Shock, more like,' Luke grimaced. 'And I didn't meet Marilou at the restaurant, I didn't meet her at all. I haven't seen her since Tuesday.'

'But she said—Maybe I misunderstood her.' She had been fooled by the other woman! Marilou had sensed that Luke's interest in her wasn't as impersonal as it should have been, and decided to warn her off. And she had fallen for it! She had responded like a child, had changed all her plans, had accepted an invitation from Luke when she hadn't really been ready for it. Damn the girl!

'You and I both know you didn't,' Luke drawled dryly, getting out of the car to open her door for her. 'I told you, Marilou is a child,' he murmured, his eyes glittering silver in the dimly lit street. 'With the reactions of a child. She realised I was attracted to you. I——'

At that moment a taxi drew into the side of the road in front of the Jaguar, and a sobbing Sally got out of the back to rush blindly past them.

CHAPTER SEVEN

'I THINK that particular big girl just learnt of her mistake,' Luke broke the stunned silence that had followed Sally's flight into the building.

Lori flashed him an angry look. 'You don't have to sound so smug about it!' She was torn between rushing to be with Sally and telling this man what she thought of him. The latter won. 'Just because one of your sex has once again made a fool of one of mine there's no reason to——'

'Steady, Lori,' he warned gruffly. 'Your friend has been hurt, and I'm sorry about that, but that's no reason for you to flare up at me.'

'Isn't it? Isn't it! I——'

'Kitten, please . . .!' His lips claimed hers in a kiss of pure gentleness.

All the fight went out of her and she kissed him back for several minutes. Finally Luke was the one to pull back, resting his forehead on hers.

'I don't usually do my lovemaking in such a public place,' he murmured. 'And as your flat isn't exactly private either, I think we should postpone this.'

Lori pulled away from him, once again angry with herself for responding. 'Indefinitely!'

'Lori——'

'I have to go to Sally,' she told him stiltedly. 'Thank you for a nice evening. I had a good time.'

'Kitten——'

'I have to go,' she insisted firmly. 'Perhaps you could

113

call me tomorrow?' She knew by the widening of his eyes that he wasn't used to being dismissed in this way, and the knowledge filled her with satisfaction. She had to keep him off guard all the time, must never let him feel as if he controlled her. 'Goodnight, Luke,' she added coolly, and walked away.

She knew he hadn't moved, could feel his gaze boring into her back as she walked steadily into the building, calmly pressing the button for the lift and stepping inside to turn towards the entrance doors, aware that Luke still stood on the pavement outside.

He looked very alone in that moment, a lone figure standing in the street. And then she hardened her heart, and turned away as the lift doors closed. Luke never had any need to be alone, not while there were willing girls like Marilou about!

Sally was in the bedroom, lying on the bed, still sobbing as if her heart were broken. As indeed Lori suspected it was!

'Sally?' she sat on the edge of the bed. 'Sally, what is it?'

For several more moments Sally continued to sob, then she turned over, her mascara running darkly down her cheeks, pain showing in her deep blue eyes.

'Is Dave ill?' she prompted.

'Ill?' Sally repeated bitterly, sitting up to brush the tears from her cheeks. 'I wish he were. And I wish I could have been the cause of it!'

'Tell me,' Lori encouraged softly.

'Dave has someone else,' Sally choked. 'He was seeing her even before he started going out with me!'

This was so much worse than she had imagined, although Dave's flirting with herself had pointed to his interest in other women besides Sally. Her heart went out to her friend. 'How did you find out?'

Sally gave a bitter laugh, standing up to pace the room. 'He told me,' she revealed scornfully, tears still glittering in her eyes. 'I told you he asked me to move in with him?' She drew in a ragged breath. 'Well, when I told him tonight that I wasn't sure I wanted to do that he told me that it didn't matter any more, that he—that this other girl, Joanna, had already agreed to move in with him this—this weekend.' Her voice broke emotionally. 'He was only with me tonight so that he could say good—goodbye.' She began to cry again.

Lori stood up to put her arms about her friend, letting her cry it out. Dave's insensitivity had only added to her general opinion that all men were bastards. There had to be the odd exception, such as Claude and Jonathan, but Dave certainly wasn't one of them.

Sally moved away minutes later, giving a rather rueful smile. 'The irony of it is,' she said shakily. 'That if I'd agreed a week ago, two days ago, I would be the one moving in this weekend, and this girl Joanna would be the one crying now.'

'Would you rather she were?'

'God, no!' Sally said disgustedly. 'I'm upset because it's over with Dave—after all, I did think I loved him. You notice the past tense?' she scorned bitterly. 'I've been such a fool,' she shook her head. 'Yes, I'm upset,' she sighed. 'But think how much worse I would have felt if I'd moved in with him and *then* found out what a swine he is. You know we've been lovers?'

'Yes,' Lori nodded.

'Of course you do,' Sally sighed again. 'What an idiot I've been! So very stupid.'

Lori shrugged. 'You loved him.'

'And now I think I hate him,' Sally said dully. 'It's so much easier to hate than it is to love.'

She had thought that herself once, but tonight she had actually found herself liking Luke Randell at times, enjoying their discussion on the theatre and music, even liking the goodnatured arguments; only his liking for Barry Manilow had seemed out of character.

But he had soon resorted to type; his attitude had been completely callous when he spoke about Sally being hurt. Men were all the same; Luke Randell could certainly never be the exception.

She was aware of Sally crying on and off through the night, but as her friend seemed to be trying to hide her sobs she very wisely pretended to be asleep herself. Sally was already feeling humiliated enough, without anyone knowing how upset she really was.

Sally was pale and hollow-eyed the next day, but Lori insisted she eat some toast for breakfast, also making sure she had some lunch. Sally ate the food without any real appetite, but she did eat it.

'I just don't know how I could have been so stupid,' she suddenly broke the silence after lunch, previously having only answered Lori in monosyllables. 'I should have known that sex was all he was after. It's all any man's after,' she added bitterly.

Lori couldn't dispute that; she knew that it was all Luke Randell really wanted, that if she could be persuaded to give in to him now, any idea of marriage would be conveniently forgotten by him. It would be far from forgotten by him, she would see to that!

'I'm sorry,' Sally said jerkily. 'I don't mean to sound—well, I didn't exactly say no, did I?' she grimaced ruefully.

'You thought he loved you.'

'Yes,' her friend sighed. 'It isn't exactly an excuse, though, is it?'

'You don't need an excuse to express love, and that's what you were doing,' Lori pointed out.

'My parents would be scandalised,' Sally looked woebegone. 'You don't know how lucky you are, Lori, not to have parents like mine to answer to. Still, that's enough about me, how did your date with Luke Randell go last night?' To her credit, at a time when she should be off all men, Sally seemed to be genuinely interested in the answer.

Actually Lori had been wondering herself how that date had gone. At the time she had thought it had gone well, that the time she had spent in Luke's arms was just long enough for him to want more. But it was almost two o'clock in the afternoon and he hadn't even telephoned her yet.

'It was nice,' she shrugged.

'Seeing him again?'

'He didn't say,' she answered truthfully.

'He's gorgeous, though, isn't he?' Sally gave an envious sigh.

'I thought you were off men,' Lori teased, not answering the statement.

Her friend grinned. 'Not his type of man, he's in a class all his own.' She stood up restlessly. 'Let's go to the shops,' she suggested eagerly. 'There's nothing I enjoy more than trying on clothes I can't afford and then telling the assistant that nothing is suitable!'

Lori didn't know whether to go or not. If she went out with Sally she might miss Luke's call—if he did call. But then again, if he did call and received no answer it could just how him once again that she was far from always available.

'Yes, let's go.' She lightheartedly joined Sally.

They were gone over two hours. Sally treated herself to a pair of extravagantly expensive velvet trousers, something she was sure she would never actually wear, as they were too smart for casual wear, and not suitable for the office.

The telephone was ringing as they entered the flat, and Lori let Sally answer it, taking Sally's trousers through to the bedroom.

'It's Luke.' Sally came through a couple of seconds later.

'Thanks.' Lori took her time about reaching the telephone, and her tone was offhand as she picked up the receiver. 'Hello, Luke.'

'Where the hell have you been?' he growled. 'I've been calling you all afternoon!'

He was angry, very angry—which was exactly what she had wanted him to feel. 'And I've been *out* all afternoon,' she told him lightly.

'Where?'

'Really, Luke——'

'Where?' he repeated hardly.

She held back her smile. 'Just to the shops.'

'Alone?'

'No,' she answered slowly, revelling in his jealousy. 'Not alone.'

There was silence at the other end of the line for several seconds, and then Luke exploded, 'You've been out with Anderson!'

'No——'

'You have, damn you!' he rasped furiously.

She could almost visualise his face contorted with rage, with that complete lack of control where she was concerned. 'I thought we settled the matter of Jonathan last night?' she cajoled.

'No,' he bit out. 'We didn't settle anything, I realise that now. I asked you why he was kissing you, and instead of answering me *you* kissed *me*, and I forgot I'd asked the damn question!' He sounded disgusted with himself for his weakness. 'Why was he kissing you, Lori?'

'Why shouldn't he?' she dismissed.

'Because I——! Because,' he spoke more calmly, taking a deep controlling breath, 'I should be the only man in your life at the moment.'

'That sort of single-mindedness has a price,' Lori baited.

'A price I've told you I'm willing to pay!' he rasped.

'Maybe I'm not,' she dismissed.

'Meaning you'll continue to see Anderson?' Luke's voice was soft, dangerously so.

'If I want to,' she goaded.

His sharp intake of breath could clearly be heard. 'And if I asked you not to?' he said at last.

'Are you asking that?'

'Yes!'

She didn't answer for several long seconds, seeming to give the matter some thought. 'All right,' she replied huskily.

'You mean yes?' he sounded incredulous, triumphantly so.

'If that's what you want.'

'Yes, Lori, that's what I want,' he said throatily. 'Will you see me tonight?'

'I'm not sure I should leave Sally——'

'She's old enough to take care of herself, Lori,' he growled. 'I need you more than she does,' he added with a groan. 'You know I tried not to call you, don't you?' he sighed.

Pleasure shot through her at the admission. 'Then why did you?'

'Because I can't stay away from you! Tonight, Lori, I have to see you tonight. I'll pick you up at seven.' He rang off before she could refuse.

She slowly replaced the receiver, having had no intention of refusing. Luke had suffered enough for one day; she intended this revenge to be slow and sweet.

'Going out?' Sally stood in front of the mirror looking critically at the black velvet trousers she was trying on once again.

'Do you mind?' Lori frowned.

'Of course not,' Sally smiled at her in the mirror. 'Oh, I know you've stayed with me today deliberately, but I'm not the suicidal type. No, I'll be fine tonight. I can wash my hair, and——' her voice broke. 'I'm sorry, Lori.' The tears began to fall once again. 'I'm being silly.'

'I won't go out,' Lori decided. 'I'll call Luke and——'

'No, you won't,' Sally said firmly. 'Actually, I—I'm very grateful to you for staying with me today, but I'd like to be alone for a while. God, how ungrateful that sounds!' she groaned.

Not ungrateful at all; Lori knew exactly how her friend felt. When Nigel had broken their engagement she had liked to be with other people, but she had welcomed being alone too. Today she hadn't given Sally time to think; the two of them had given the flat a thorough clean this morning, and then they had been to the shops this afternoon. Now Sally needed to be alone, and she respected that.

'I understand, Sally,' she assured her softly. 'I really do. And the trousers look great!' she changed the subject.

She was still in the bedroom when Luke arrived a little before seven, and after ten minutes Sally came into the bedroom to see what was delaying her. 'He's getting impatient,' she whispered, looking like someone hounded.

'Really?' Lori continued to calmly apply the perfume

Luke had expressed a liking for. The stark white dress she wore had a dipping cowl neckline, a wide white belt at the waist, the material fitting snugly over her slender thighs. Thin shoulder straps left her arms and throat bare, and it was here that she applied the perfume.

'You look wonderful,' Sally told her. 'But he's been pacing up and down the lounge ever since he arrived—I fear for the carpet!'

Lori smiled, slowly applying her lip-gloss. 'A little delay isn't going to hurt him.'

'He doesn't look the type who appreciates being kept waiting,' her friend frowned. 'And I don't know what to talk to him about. After all, he is the new boss.'

'He's only a man for all that.' Lori slipped her silken feet into the white sandals.

Sally sat down on the bed, awestruck. 'I wish I could be as cool with men as you are. You've only been out with the man once and already you have him eating out of your hand!' She shook her head. 'How do you do it?'

Lori laughed coolly. 'I don't "do" anything, Sally. And I'm sure you're exaggerating—Luke wouldn't eat out of anyone's hand, and certainly not a woman's.'

'Well, if he isn't now, he's very close to it,' Sally decided.

Close to it wasn't good enough, not for what she had in mind. Luke's father had killed her parents and lost her Nigel for all time, and becoming Luke's wife would be payment.

Sally stood up. 'I'll tell him you're almost ready, shall I?' she prompted hopefully.

'You can tell him,' Lori nodded. 'But I'm not.'

'Lori . . .?'

'No man whose interest is really genuine would baulk at waiting twenty minutes.' She looked at the slender gold watch on her wrist. 'I still have five minutes to go.'

'He could just walk out.'

'He could,' she nodded.

'Wouldn't you care?' Sally looked scandalised. 'He looks absolutely lethal! And he smells of this aftershave that makes my toes curl.'

'Down, Rover!' Lori teased. 'He's mine, remember?'

'How could I forget?' Sally grimaced. 'Okay, I'll go and tell him you'll be out in a minute.'

'Four, to be exact.'

'By which time he *will* have worn a hole in the carpet. I just hope you have the money for a new one!'

Lori laughed with her friend, but her humour faded as soon as the door closed behind her. So Luke was impatient for her, was he? Well, he would be even more impatient by the time she had finished, and not just for her presence; he would be impatient for much more than that.

And yet that slight feeling of unease she had had last night returned. Last night she had responded to Luke quite instinctively, had found pleasure in his arms.

So she had found pleasure! Any number of experienced men could have evoked the same response from even the most unwilling of women. And yet that disquietening feeling remained, and her eyes were guarded as she went out to greet him.

Desire blazed in the light grey eyes like a molten fire, his gaze caressing as it slowly ran over the softness of her curves clearly shown beneath the clinging white dress.

Luke did indeed look devastating, his black evening trousers and smoky grey velvet jacket superbly tailored across his broad shoulders and athletic body.

Lori was the only one aware of Sally's mumbled words before she hastily disappeared into the bedroom, and Luke held Lori's gaze as he slowly came towards her.

'Did you do it on purpose?' He stood only inches away from her, the warmth of his body reaching out to her.

'Do what?' Her voice was husky, her eyes demure as she looked up at him from beneath luscious lashes.

'Keep me waiting.' His hands moved to touch her bare arms. 'You knew how badly I wanted to see you tonight.'

'Did I?'

'You know you did.' His eyes darkened. 'Kitten . . .!' he moaned before his lips parted hers.

After several seconds she broke the contact. 'Sally's in the other room,' she murmured pointedly as Luke still held her, the throbbing of his body telling her that it was as well Sally was in the flat.

'Yes,' he moved away with a sigh. 'We're going to be late as it is.'

'Late?' she frowned.

'I thought we could go and see Claude before going to dinner.'

Now she felt guilty about deliberately keeping him waiting. 'I'll just say goodbye to Sally,' she said stiltedly.

'How is she?' Luke asked once they were in the Jaguar and on their way to the hospital.

'Hurting,' Lori told him bluntly.

'Is it over with her boy-friend?'

'Yes.'

'Hey,' he chided gently, putting out a hand to entwine his fingers with hers, '*I* wasn't the one who hurt your friend!'

She snatched her hand out of his. 'I'm sorry,' she said abruptly, 'I just don't like to see Sally hurt.'

'I'm hurting,' he told her huskily.

It was an admission she knew he didn't like making,

because it was against his nature to admit to any weakness. 'I'm sorry,' she said again.

'Are you?' Bitterness entered his voice. 'What game are you playing with me, Lori?' he bit out.

'Game?' she echoed sharply, her expression guarded. 'I don't understand.'

He looked grim, his expression taut. 'You know I want you, you know how I feel about you. I wouldn't advise you to use those feelings to your advantage.' His voice was hard with warning.

'What do you mean?' She moistened her lips nervously.

'Don't treat my love as a weakness, kitten,' he advised softly, dangerously so.

'Love, Luke?' Her brows rose.

'You know damn well I'm in love with you!' he rasped, a pulse beating erratically at his jaw.

It was the first time he had mentioned love, and she felt a surge of satisfaction that he had said it now, her lashes lowering to shield her elation.

'You did know, didn't you?' he frowned at her silence.

'You never mentioned it,' she said demurely.

'But I thought——'

'There's a vast difference between loving and wanting, Luke,' she drawled. 'And you've only ever spoken of the latter.'

'But I thought you would know!'

'How could I?'

'Oh hell!' he scowled. 'And we're at the hospital now.' He turned in his seat to look at her. 'We'll talk about this later?'

'If you like,' Lori nodded coolly.

'I like,' he confirmed gruffly, gently touching the creamy texture of her cheek.

Claude's expression brightened when they walked into his room together. He was looking much better than when they had last seen him, and was sitting up in the bed, his colour almost normal.

'Ruth's already left for the evening,' he told them, switching off the television set.

'We would have been here earlier ourselves,' Luke drawled, his arm about Lori's waist in a show of possession. 'But you know what women are, they think they have to paint the lily—when we would much rather have the lily without any adornment at all,' he mocked her.

'Ah, but Lori paints so nicely,' Claude smiled at his teasing. 'I can also see that her temper is rising nicely. You're familiar with her temper?'

'Very,' Luke taunted. 'Actually, it isn't so much a temper as a steely determination,' he added thoughtfully.

Lori looked at him sharply. She might be coming to know this man, but he also seemed to be analysing her—and coming up with the right answers. She would have to be wary that he didn't discover the whole truth about her before she was ready for him to.

Claude laughed softly. 'Am I to take it this— togetherness is a regular thing?'

'Yes,' Lori was the one to answer him. 'And after Luke saying he didn't agree with a close working as well as outside relationship!' she did some taunting of her own.

Lukes eyes were amused, his fingers bit into her waist in a warning pinch. 'I believe I said between husband and wife,' he mocked her blushes. 'Although I'm working on that,' he told the other man softly.

'Really?' Claude's interest deepened.

'Very much so,' Luke nodded. 'But she's a tough one to convince.'

'Do you really think that?' Lori asked later that night as they sat in his car outside her home.

They had gone from the hospital to a quiet restaurant, where the food was once again excellent, the conversation even more so. Luke had set out to entertain—and had succeeded.

Lori's mood had been very mellow by the time they went on to the club, where she and Luke danced silently in each other's arms for almost two hours, hardly moving, Luke's lips occasionally travelling the length of her throat, searching each contour of her face, his breathing soft and shallow as he told her how beautiful she was, how much he desired her.

The latter she had been well aware of; it was the loving she was more interested in, which was why she was probing his emotions now.

'Think what, my darling?' Luke held her tightly in his arms, his eyes a silver glaze from the heated kisses they had been exchanging for the last ten minutes, Lori explaining that she would rather not take him up to the flat, not when Sally was feeling so emotionally fragile. She also knew Luke would never make love to her here—her safeguard against her lowering resistance towards him.

'That I'm tough to convince?' She had no idea how lovely she looked in that moment, her hair loose about her shoulders, her eyes a deep sparkling brown, her mouth a deep red despite being bare of lip-gloss, witness to Luke's passion.

'About marriage?' He sat back slightly. 'You haven't made it easy so far.'

'Would you rather I had?' She touched the bareness of his chest, having unbuttoned his shirt minutes earlier, feeling his skin firm to the touch, sensually so.

'Maybe a little more than you did,' he nodded. 'I've

never asked a woman to marry me before, and it's a little off-putting to find she doesn't even take me seriously.'

'You were a little unorthodox in the beginning, Luke,' she chided softly. 'But I'm starting to take you seriously now.' Her lips travelled the hardness of his chest, loving his instant reaction to the caress.

'You are?' His voice was gruff.

'Yes.' She looked up at him.

'Don't stop now!' He kissed her temple.

'You're greedy,' she laughed teasingly.

'Where you're concerned, yes.'

'And Marilou?'

He shook his head, buttoning his shirt as she moved away from him. 'That young madam was on a plane for home first thing this morning—I saw to that.'

It hadn't been a very pleasant experience for the younger girl, if Luke's grim expression was anything to go by. 'You didn't approve of your surprise, then?' she asked lightly.

'Not at all. And I made sure she knew that.'

'She liked you.' Lori could afford to be generous now that the other girl was back in America.

'And I'm in love with you,' he told her deeply. 'Next to that I'm afraid little girls like Marilou don't mean a thing.'

'Keep telling me,' she encouraged throatily. 'Perhaps I'll come to believe it.'

'I hope so. We'll meet tomorrow?'

'I usually visit my aunt on Sundays.'

'Let me come with you,' he suggested reasonably.

Lori blinked. 'Come with me?'

'Why not?' he nodded. 'It's time I met your family, and this aunt is your family, isn't she?'

'Yes.' She frowned; the prospect of Luke and Aunt

Jessie meeting was not something she had taken into consideration. Her aunt might be eighty years of age, but she was far from being senile. If she should realise Luke was Jacob P. Randell's son she could just add two and two together and come up with the right answer.

In the early days after the trial, Lori had made no secret of her hatred of the famous lawyer, had often expressed a wish to 'get back at him'. Aunt Jessie would only have to become suspicious of her real reason for seeing Luke and she could ruin the whole thing for her; not even the fact that Nigel's marriage had opened up the old wound would influence her aunt's decision to tell Luke the truth.

But she could understand Luke wanting to meet her aunt, and it would make her own suggestion of meeting his father all the more acceptable when the time came.

'All right,' she finally agreed. 'But Aunt Jessie is very old, and she—she sometimes rambles.' Oh, Aunt Jessie, forgive me, she pleaded silently. Her aunt had never rambled in her life, and even at eighty years of age could out-think a lot of younger people, herself included.

'I don't mind that, darling,' Luke smiled. 'She's your aunt, and you love her.'

'You won't mind if she—if she's very blunt?'

'After your evasive tactics I'll welcome it,' he grinned. 'Now come and kiss me goodnight,' and he held out his arms to her.

Her kiss was reserved, knowing that earlier she had once again responded to him. He ruefully accepted the way she held back now, and sat back in his own seat.

'I'd better go in,' Lori told him breathlessly.

'Yes, I think you'd better—before I decide to try and persuade you to come home with me.'

'You wouldn't succeed.'

'I know it,' he grimaced. 'But I might have enjoyed trying. What time shall I call for you tomorrow?'

She told him, getting out of the car to let him walk her to the door. Sally had already gone to bed when she got inside, although she had left the light on in the lounge for her.

Lori went into the bedroom as quietly as she could after her wash, not wanting to disturb her friend if she was already asleep. She wasn't; she was sitting up in bed to switch on the lamp that stood on the table between the two beds.

'Have a good evening?'

'Very good.' Lori hung her dress up in the wardrobe, knowing that she spoke the truth. It had been a good evening.

'I called Dave's flat this evening,' Sally told her slowly, almost reluctantly, it seemed.

Lori's eyes widened. 'What did he say?'

'Nothing,' her friend said dully. 'He wasn't there. Joanna answered the telephone.' Sally held back her tears with difficulty.

Lori climbed into the opposite bed, frowning. 'Did she know who you were?'

'No, she didn't seem to. And I didn't tell her either.' Sally lay back on her pillow staring up at the ceiling. 'I found I didn't hate Dave enough to do that to him. I'm sure she'll find out the truth about him in time.'

Lori wasn't so sure she would have had the same forbearance if it had been her!

Long after Sally had fallen asleep she lay awake, worried as to the outcome of Luke's meeting with Aunt Jessie tomorrow.

CHAPTER EIGHT

SALLY had decided to go and spend the day with her family when she got up the next morning, leaving straight after breakfast. In the circumstances Lori thought it was probably the best thing for her. Sally came from a big family, four brothers and a sister; the main reason she had wanted to move into a flat of her own. But Lori knew that when one of them was in trouble or unhappy the others closed ranks about them. Sally would feel a lot better for being with that closeness today.

Luke arrived just after eleven, casually but smartly dressed, his grey trousers and grey-checked jacket superbly tailored, a black silk shirt fitting tautly across his chest and flat stomach.

'Will I do?' he asked as she looked up at him.

'You know you will,' she smiled, knowing he had dressed to please her aunt, wanting to make a good impression.

'You will too,' he said throatily, his eyes silver-grey, very intense. 'Come here,' he instructed softly.

She held back, nervous of the response he was beginning to evoke in her whenever he touched her. 'I think we should be going,' she said lightly.

'We have time for you to kiss me hello.' He drew her into his arms, bending his head to claim her mouth in a kiss that seemed to draw the very soul from her body.

Her lips opened to his as she felt his hands moving over her caressingly. The tan dress she wore was of a thin silky material, and the heat of his body was clearly discernible to her.

Lori clutched on to his shoulders as a familiar warmth began to invade her body, her head bent back as his kiss deepened to fierceness, his hands now fevered on her body, caressing her from breast to thigh. The zip on her dress slowly slid down her spine, and Luke's hands followed the same path, curving her to him.

'Kitten, I love you,' he groaned, slipping the dress off one shoulder to explore its creamy curve, smoothing the material down to her waist as he claimed one peaked breast between his pleasure-giving lips.

She leant against him weakly, moving with him as if in a dream as he sat down in an armchair to pull her on to his lap, his mouth at once returning to the throbbing nub of her breast, his tongue on her nipple shooting spasms of sensation through to her fingertips. Without even being aware of it she was moaning low in her throat.

'That's it, kitten,' he encouraged huskily. 'Purr for me, my darling.'

She *was* purring, there was no other way to describe that almost animalistic moan of pleasure she was giving, and it shocked her to the root of her being that she was allowing Luke to touch her so intimately—and enjoying it.

She struggled to sit up, standing to refasten her dress, finding it impossible to even look at Luke, although she knew he had been as affected as she had, his heart beating swiftly as he caressed her, his thighs surging wildly against her.

'I love you, Lori,' he said suddenly, straightening the darkness of his hair with one hand. 'I love you, we're both adults, and we have no need to be embarrassed about the fact that we have a fiery effect on each other.'

His gaze was intent. 'Did you make love with your ex-fiancé?'

Lori stiffened, moving to the mirror to brush her hair and re-apply her lipstick, surprised that her reflection could still look back at her so calmly when she was so angry inside. How dared Luke Randell question her about her relationship with Nigel? He had no right to question her about anything, least of all *Nigel!*

'Lori?' Luke prompted huskily, coming to stand directly behind her, looking dark and dangerous in the mirror.

She forced warmth into her eyes. 'Have I asked you about your past lovers, Luke?' she attempted to tease.

His mouth thinned, his eyes suddenly icy. 'This is different——'

'Why?' she demanded to know. 'Because I was engaged to him? Really, Luke, a sexual relationship doesn't come along with the engagement ring,' she scorned.

His mouth twisted. 'I didn't think it did,' he rasped. 'I just have to know!'

'Why?' Her anger was beginning to show now. 'What good would it do——'

'I have to know, Lori!' His eyes glittered, his body tensed as if about to spring.

'No!' Her tone was sharp. 'No, I didn't make love with my ex-fiancé. Are you satisfied now?'

He heaved a deep sigh, as if he had been holding his breath as he waited for her answer. 'Yes, that satisfies me. I can't help my jealousy, Lori,' he rasped. 'The thought of you with any other man but me drives me insane.'

She collected her jacket from the bedroom, looking at him coolly. 'I said I didn't make love with my fiancé,' she told him as she slipped the brown jacket on over the tan dress. 'But that was five years ago, Luke,' her head went back in challenge. 'I was nineteen, very naïve, and now I'm a woman.'

'With a woman's needs?' he rasped.

'Exactly,' she nodded.

'I don't believe you.' He shook his head with arrogant confidence. 'I remember a double-edged conversation we had once about sailing——'

'I remember it too,' her mouth twisted mockingly. 'I also told you I'd tried it.'

'Once!'

'Several times,' she bit out stubbornly. 'Now could we please leave. My aunt is expecting us at twelve.'

'I haven't finished yet——'

'And I don't want to discuss this any further.' Her voice was steely. 'I've been out with you a couple of times, I don't have to explain myself to you about anything. If you would rather not go to see my aunt——'

'I'm coming with you!' His hand gripped her arm, his expression forbidding as they went down to the car.

Oh, she could have told Luke that she and Nigel had decided to wait until they were married before making love—a marriage that wasn't to be. She could also have told him that she hadn't allowed any man near enough since to even approach a physical relationship. But she saw no reason to tell him any of that, considering it her own affair what she had done before she met him, and no one else's. Luke was just like all men—he liked to gain experience himself, but when it came to the woman he loved she had to be chaste. In this day and age of reliable contraception and availability, that was asking a lot of any woman. It was certainly asking too much of her to tell him the truth!

But if they made the journey to see her aunt in stony

silence, Luke's expression grim, then she could see he was visibly trying to break the mood as they walked to her aunt's tiny flat. It was a battle within himself he seemed to be having difficulty with.

'To hell with it!' he snapped suddenly as they stood outside her aunt's door, and turned to pull Lori into his arms to kiss her firmly on the mouth.

Lori's eyes widened at this unexpected onslaught, but she was too surprised to fight it.

Luke's eyes glittered with satisfaction as he moved back. 'I don't give a damn if you've had a hundred lovers, I'm still going to marry you!'

'Hardly a hundred, Luke!' She regained her composure with effort, looking about them selfconsciously, although the hallway appeared to be deserted except for themselves. Her lip-gloss was once again non-existent, her mouth swollen from the passion of the kiss she had just received.

'Don't push it, kitten,' Luke warned softly. 'Or I'll be sorely tempted to take you away from here and make you do more than purr!'

His mocking laughter followed her hasty entrance into the flat, and she knew he was amused by her evasion of being in his arms. But that part of her plan was spiralling out of control, becoming so that she *couldn't* control it. Each time Luke made love to her he seemed to wear her resistance down a little bit more, and this last time it had taken tremendous effort to break the spell. They had been at the flat, without fear of interruption from others in the immediate future, and she had found just how dangerous that was. She would have to do what she had done last night, try to make sure they were never alone in places where he could do more than kiss her.

So much for her aversion to him! He was slowly

proving that to be untrue, and despite her despisal of
the Randell family, Luke's physical effect on her was
growing stronger.

Her aunt was in the process of watering her plants
when they entered, and without turning she barked,
'You're late again. Really, Lorraine, your time-keeping
is atrocious! What your boss thinks of you I have no
idea,' she tutted.

Lori gave Luke a rueful shrug, seeing by the amused
raising of his eyebrows that he was already captivated
by the elderly lady. No doubt her bluntness appealed to
him!

'He thinks,' Luke said slowly, teasingly, smiling as
her aunt slowly turned to look at him, 'that she's the
most beautiful woman he's ever seen—and that she
needn't come in until lunchtime if she doesn't want to,'
he drawled.

'I'll remember that,' she warned softly.

'As long as I'm the one she spends the morning with,'
he added softly.

Aunt Jessie was looking at him critically, obviously
liking what she saw, although she looked a little worried.
'I thought you said Mr Hammond was married—with a
grown up son,' she said in a scandalised voice.

'He is, and he has,' Lori said with amusement; it was
not hard to imagine Luke's reaction to having a son of
Paul's age—there were only a few years between them!

Aunt Jessie looked at Luke again, keen interest in her
faded blue eyes. And Lori knew why. The only other
man she had ever introduced to her aunt was Nigel, and
with her aunt's dislike of him that hadn't been a great
success. Her aunt didn't seem to have the same aversion
to Luke. It piqued her a little that her aunt should have
disapproved of Nigel so strongly and yet should
actually seem to like Luke.

'Then this isn't him,' her aunt realised. 'Is he Jonathan?'

Lori was aware of a sudden tension about Luke; she knew that he was still jealous of any mention of the other man. 'No, this isn't Jonathan either, Aunt Jessie,' she smiled. 'This is my new boss, Luke Randell,' she said the last tentatively, watching her aunt for any sign of recognition of Luke's surname. There didn't appear to be any as the two of them shook hands, Luke handing her aunt the fuchsia he had bought for her on the way there.

Her aunt seemed pleased by the gesture, and smiled at him coyly. 'You're so kind.'

Lori's eyes widened at her aunt's almost flirtatious manner. She really did like Luke!

'Not at all,' he returned smoothly. 'If lunch is as delicious as it smells, the plant is the least I could do!'

'Lorraine can go and check on the food while we sit down and have a chat,' her aunt said imperiously.

'Oh, she can, can she?' Lori smiled.

'Yes, she can.' Aunt Jessie looked at her over the top of her glasses.

She couldn't help laughing at that stern expression. 'I stopped being intimidated by those looks years ago,' she chuckled. 'But I'll go and check on lunch anyway. I brought a trifle for dessert.' She carried the dish through to the adjoining kitchen, putting her head around the side of the door just in time to see her aunt and Luke getting comfortable in opposite chairs. 'And no telling him any of my dark secrets!' It was a teasing warning, but one with an underlying strength she knew her aunt couldn't miss.

'You don't have any dark secrets,' Aunt Jessie dismissed lightly. 'Except maybe that awful man you were once engaged to,' she added thoughtfully.

'Aunt Jessie!' Lori gasped indignantly.

Amusement glittered in grey eyes as Luke sat forward in his seat. 'Tell me more,' he invited the elderly lady.

'Well, he——'

'Aunt Jessie, please!' she groaned, determined that Luke shouldn't know anything about Nigel. So far he had just been another man she could taunt Luke with, the truth of her break-up with Nigel would show she was the one who had been scorned. 'Tell Luke what a horrible little girl I was, tell him how well I did at school, but please leave Nigel out of it!' She raised dark brows at her aunt.

'All right,' her aunt accepted her plea. 'Now go and check on lunch before it burns,' she ordered.

Lori could hear Luke's deep-throated chuckle as she put the vegetables on to cook and took the meat out of the oven. Whatever Aunt Jessie was telling him, he was enjoying himself.

He seemed to do so through lunch too; he and her aunt were almost like conspirators as they teased her.

'Now I hope you're going to be kind to my Lorraine,' her aunt warned him as they prepared to take their leave. 'Underneath this tough exterior is a little girl who's been hurt very badly in the past.'

Lori paled. 'Aunt Jessie——'

'I intend being very kind to her,' Luke assured the elderly lady softly. 'As kind as any husband can be to the woman he loves.'

'Luke!'

'Be quiet, Lorraine!' her aunt instructed impatiently. 'If you have nothing more sensible to say than gasping our names in that ridiculous way then don't talk at all.' She looked over her glasses at Luke. 'So you intend marrying my great-niece, do you?'

He nodded. 'As soon as she accepts my proposal.'

'Giving you trouble, is she?'

'Very much so,' he smiled, his gaze mocking Lori's barely held temper.

'You look strong enough to handle her,' Aunt Jessie said with satisfaction. 'That other pip-squeak——'

'Aunt Jessie, we really do have to go now,' Lori interrupted softly. So far, in the circumstances, the day had gone very smoothly, but if her aunt started talking about Nigel there was no telling what she might say.

'She hates me talking about him,' her aunt told Luke. 'I'm not surprised. He was no good for her. Didn't have the backbone of a——'

'Aunt Jessie!' Lori sighed her exasperation with the elderly lady.

'We should be on our way,' Luke put in smoothly, his arm about Lori's waist as he guided her to the door. 'I've enjoyed meeting you, Jessie,' he smiled. 'I hope I'll soon be able to call you Aunt Jessie as Lori does.'

Lori had barely been able to hide her surprise when she came back from the kitchen to find Luke calling her aunt by her first name, and her aunt returning the compliment. Her aunt had known Nigel for almost a year, and yet she had always insisted that he call her Miss Chisholm. Luke seemed to have achieved the impossible, that of charming her aunt within a matter of minutes.

'I liked her,' Luke announced on the drive back to town.

'Maybe the two of you should get married!' she said waspishly.

His mouth tightened. 'I quite like older women,' he rasped. 'But I believe you're doing your aunt a disservice by talking about her in this way.'

She blushed at the rebuke, knowing it was deserved. 'She liked you too,' she told him huskily. 'And I'm sorry, I didn't mean to be bitchy.'

He shrugged his dismissal of the subject. 'I gather she didn't take to your ex-fiancé in the same way?'

'No,' Lori acknowledged tightly.

'Why not?'

She shrugged. 'I have no idea. Maybe because he didn't try so hard to make an impression,' she added nastily, unfairly.

Luke's face darkened once again. 'I didn't try to make an impression either,' he snapped. 'Why do I sometimes get the impression that *you* still don't like me?' he said slowly.

Lori flushed. She was allowing her temper to reveal her true feelings towards this man, and that would never do. At the moment he was deeply in love with her, but if he should ever guess at her plan she had no doubt that love would turn to blazing anger. Luke showed her the gentle side of his nature, but she had also seen him blisteringly angry, and he could be formidable then.

'You're imagining things,' she told him lightly.

'Am I?' he said grimly.

'Of course.' She deliberately let her hand rest on his thigh, feeling his instant response. 'Why else would I go out with you if I didn't like you?'

'Why else, indeed?' he murmured thoughtfully.

'Don't let's ruin the day by arguing again, Luke,' she said pleadingly, her eyes softly encouraging as she looked at him.

He seemed to draw back from anger with an effort. 'We do seem to argue rather a lot,' he said lightly. 'Do you suppose we'll argue like this when we're married?'

She smiled at his arrogance. 'I haven't accepted you yet.'

'No,' he grimaced. 'But I'll just keep asking until you do.'

'Don't you think I should meet your family before we decide on anything as important as marriage?' she suggested slowly, as if the idea had just occurred to her. 'After all, you've met Aunt Jessie.'

'I only have my father now,' he told her harshly, his expression grim. 'And I see no reason for you to meet him.'

Her eyes widened; the rift between father and son appeared to be wider than Claude had first implied it was. And that couldn't help her plan for revenge at all. 'Why not?' she asked.

Luke didn't seem as if he were really listening to her, lost in thoughts of his own, the harshness of his voice seconds earlier now reflected in his face, his grey eyes icy, his nostrils flaring, his lips compressed into a thin angry line.

Lori's own thoughts were chaotic. Surely she hadn't come this far, encouraged this man even though she despised him, only to be thwarted at the end by his own anger with his father! She wouldn't be put off now; she had come too far to baulk at the end.

'Why not?' she prompted at Luke's continued silence.

'I've seen him once since I got back from the States,' he told her abruptly, 'on the Sunday following Paul's wedding, and I don't see any reason to repeat the visit in the near future.'

This couldn't be happening, not after all she had gone through just to get this far. 'I would like to meet him, Luke,' she said stubbornly.

'The great Jacob P. Randell!' he scorned.

'Your father,' she corrected softly at his bitterness.

'He's never been a father to me,' Luke rasped tautly. 'Not like other children had fathers. As a child I rarely saw him. My mother lived in the country because she preferred it, my father spent most of his time in

London. It was all he could do to spare the time to come to the occasional open day at my boarding-school,' he revealed bitterly, his eyes shadowed with remembered pain.

'And yet you became a lawyer too.'

He gave a bitter laugh. 'At the time I didn't have much choice, and to be honest, I didn't really want one. The son of Jacob Randell couldn't really enter any other career but law. For a while I even admired him—professionally, thought about entering the partnership he ran so successfully.'

'Why didn't you?' she prompted huskily, knowing just exactly how successful Jacob Randell had been at his profession.

Luke's mouth twisted with distaste. 'Let's just say I became disenchanted with his way of doing things.'

'And that's when you went to America?'

'Yes.'

'So you don't intend I should meet him?'

'Is it that important to you that you should?' he scowled.

She swallowed hard. 'Yes.'

'Then I'll call him,' Luke told her abruptly. 'Next week. Maybe we could see him some time over the weekend.'

Lori nodded, hardly able to believe she was this close to meeting the man she had hated for twelve years. 'I'd like that,' she nodded.

'I don't know why. Just remember,' he ground out, 'that it's me you'll be marrying, not my father!'

She suppressed a shiver of revulsion at the thought of being married to Jacob P. Randell, and eagerly accepted Luke's suggestion that they stop for dinner somewhere—not a quiet restaurant this time but a noisy club, the dining tables placed around the side of the space for dancing, the cabaret act, a sultry girl singer, up on the stage behind this.

Luke threw himself into the enjoyment of the evening almost as if he wanted to banish the thought of his father from his mind, as if the thoughts she had evoked earlier by her questions had revived memories he would rather forget.

Her protests that they weren't really dressed for such a place were quickly overridden by Luke's determination. The reckless mood he was in it was easier to fall in with his wishes than argue with him.

For the first time in their acquaintance she noticed several covetous looks being given in her direction, beautiful bejewelled women aged from twenty to fifty! Even casually dressed as he was now Luke was still a devastatingly handsome man, tall and commanding, with the blatant good looks of a film star—and there were already enough of them here! Lori had been taken aback to see several well-known film stars and television personalities either gyrating on the dance floor or sitting at their tables. Luke seemed unaffected by the presence of such people.

They were dancing slowly in each other's arms, their dinner over, when a woman suddenly shouted Luke's name, dragging her reluctant partner over to where Luke had stopped dancing to turn and look at her, his arm about Lori's waist.

'Good God—Margot!' Luke greeted familiarly, smiling his pleasure.

The woman wasn't so staid about showing her pleasure, launching herself excitedly into his arms, kissing the surprised Luke soundly on the mouth.

Lori stood back as she recognised the other woman, her face very white. Margot Phillips—Nigel's young sister! And it looked as if she knew Luke very well indeed!

CHAPTER NINE

THE other girl had only been sixteen when Lori last met her, a precocious little brat, taking an instant dislike to Nigel's girl-friend when she came home from boarding-school to meet Lori at the engagement party.

That dislike had been reciprocated, Margot's verbal attack on her when they had chanced to be alone precluding there ever being a chance of friendship between the two of them.

But that had all been five years ago, and the promise of Margot's beauty had blossomed into a striking attraction; her hair was as blonde as her brother's, her blue eyes full of sparkling humour, the red pout of her mouth having made contact with Luke's, the tall perfection of body curved against him.

Yes, Margot had grown into a very beautiful woman—and she could bring the whole world down about Lori's ears. With just a few words this woman, a woman she knew to be totally vindictive—a trait she had no doubt inherited from her father—could tell Luke exactly who she was and ruin her life once again.

'It's so good to see you again!' Margot was beaming up at Luke, totally forgetting the young man who was her partner for the evening. 'When did you get back from the States?'

'Last month,' Luke drawled, pulling Lori forward pointedly.

Margot eyed her curiously—and without recognition! Her eyes were coolly appraising, showing no sign of recognition at all.

'Margot,' the man at her side gained her attention, 'the others are leaving now.'

She gave him an irritated glare, looking towards a table where several people were getting to their feet in preparation for leaving. Lori followed the other woman's line of vision with a feeling akin to horror, dreading seeing that Nigel made up one of the party. But of course he wouldn't, he was on his honeymoon!

. 'I have to go,' Margot told Luke regretfully, giving Lori another cold look. 'Call me. You have our number?'

'Yes,' Luke smiled.

Margot kissed him on the lips once again. 'Lovely to have you back, Luke.' She nodded distantly to Lori before allowing her partner to guide her out of the club.

Lori's hands felt damp with perspiration as she turned to face Luke, weakly suggesting that they leave too, having the excuse of work in the morning for this early end to their evening.

'Margot's enthusiastic greeting didn't bother you, did it?' Luke frowned at her silence as they drove home.

'Of course not,' she said sharply.

'I've known her since she was a child,' Luke explained.

That was what she had been afraid of! It had never occurred to her that Luke could know Margot Phillips, and if he had known the other woman since she was a child then it followed that he also knew Nigel and his parents.

'I was at law school with her brother Nigel,' he added by way of explanation. 'He and I were quite good friends in those days.'

This was getting worse! He actually knew Nigel very well too. Lori had a feeling of things starting to close in about her.

'He got married a couple of weeks ago, although I didn't go,' Luke added. 'Did you see it in the newspapers?'

'No,' her denial was strangulated.

'It seems that all my friends are getting married, and when I had thought they were all die-hard bachelors! Of course Nigel was going to marry once before,' his mouth tightened, 'but it never took place.'

Lori had stiffened at his mention of Nigel's previous marriage plans, the hardness of his tone seeming to indicate that he had disapproved of Nigel's last choice of bride as strongly as Charles Phillips had. 'Why?' she asked coldly.

'I have no idea,' he lied—and Lori knew he lied. Luke knew exactly why that first marriage had never taken place. 'I hardly recognised Margot,' he mused. 'She must have been about fourteen the last time I saw her. How delightfully you women grow up!'

'I noticed,' she said tightly, still angry at his prejudice.

Luke laughed softly. 'Margot is a child to me, Lori.'

'So was Marilou,' she mocked dryly, knowing he was enjoying what he thought was a display of jealousy. She had wanted to know how well he knew the Phillips, and now that she did know she wished she didn't. 'They can't all be children, Luke. And Marilou acted very *un*like a child. So did Margot, for that matter.'

'I wish you would act so impetuously,' he said drily.

'Maybe one day I'll surprise you.'

'I'll live for the day!'

She would surprise him, and one day soon. But it would be far from the surprise he wanted.

Lori went out with Luke three evenings that week, refusing to see him every night, going to the cinema with Sally one evening, and spending the other one doing her washing. Luke treated the latter refusal with amusement, the evening she claimed to be with Sally, suspiciously. He seemed to suspect her of seeing another man that evening.

They went to see Claude on Tuesday evening, calling to see him again on Saturday before going on to the theatre to see the new Tom Stoppard play, and going out to supper afterwards.

Luke drank his wine slowly, looking at Lori over the rim of the glass. 'I called my father today,' he told her softly.

Her hand shook slightly as she carried her own wine glass to her lips. He hadn't mentioned whether or not he intended calling his father, and she hadn't like to pressurise him into it, leaving it to her cool behaviour to tell him she was still undecided about marrying him.

In fact she had been very cool towards him the last few days, never being alone with him for longer than it could be helped, a fact he seemed very well aware of, for his mood was explosive.

This move had been made as much out of self-preservation as to keep Luke at arm's length. When they had parted Sunday evening she had found once again how weak she was where his kisses were concerned, had almost succumbed to his plea to go to his home with him. Her weakness towards this man frightened her, and she was very wisely avoiding being alone with him in potentially dangerous situations. With Luke there seemed to be all too many of them.

Now it seemed that he had been in touch with his father after all.

'What did he say?' she asked softly.

'Not a lot,' Luke sighed, putting his glass down. 'But then he never does,' he grimaced.

'Did you—mention me?' Lori held her breath, feeling a tingling down her spine at the thought of meeting her adversary after all these years.

'Of course I mentioned you,' Luke said sharply. 'You were the only reason I called him.'

Luke's temper had been very frayed the last few days, and she knew it was frustration over her that was causing it. She felt sure this was the first time in years that Luke had gone to the trouble of actually having to woo a girl. It was certainly the first time he had waited this length of time to make love to one of his women. Luke had never been serious about a woman before, he had told her so, and so the women he had been out with in the past had been chosen because they had no interest in marriage either. Abstinance certainly didn't improve his temper!

'We're going to see him tomorrow,' Luke snapped at her silence.

'I don't remember being asked.' She looked at him with cool brown eyes.

'And you aren't going to be,' he said angrily. 'It was your idea, the least you can do is come with me.'

'I——'

'Let's leave.' He stood up abruptly to pay the bill.

'Luke——'

'I can't stand it any more,' he told her through gritted teeth, glaring at the manager as he came to enquire whether there had been anything wrong with their half-eaten meal. The poor man retreated under an icy grey stare, shrugging his shoulders ruefully.

Colour winged in Lori's cheeks as they left the restaurant, sure that everyone could guess the reason Luke was hurrying her from the room. She had never felt so embarrassed in her life!

'That was unforgivable!' She turned to him when

they got outside, pulling her silver-coloured shawl on over the clinging black gown she wore. 'I've never been so humiliated in my life!' She got into the Jaguar as he held the door open for her.

Luke's expression was grim as he got in beside her, his face stormy as he drove the car though the busy streets.

'Luke, did you hear me——'

'Yes,' he bit out unapproachably.

Lori sensed a definite change in his mood, no longer in control of this situation—at least, not as far as tonight was concerned. Luke had come to the end of his tenacious restraint, and it appeared this unwanted visit to his father was the cause of it.

'If you would rather not visit your father then we won't go.' She held her breath as she waited for his answer, knowing she had to make the offer, feeling compelled to.

'The arrangements have been made now,' he told her tersely, not even glancing at her, his face rigid. 'I've told my father about you, and he's looking forward to meeting you.'

And she was looking forward to seeing Jacob Randell once again. He had been the man she feared when she was younger, the man she hated as she grew older, and in her mind he had grown to gigantic proportions, out of all context with a normal human being. She remembered him as looking like an older version of Luke, but that had been twelve years ago. He would be seventy years of age now, but no less formidable, she felt sure.

'That's nice,' she said without sincerity.

'So you'll come with me tomorrow?'

'If that's what you want.'

'What I want doesn't seem to matter a whole lot in

our relationship,'Luke snapped. 'Is Sally at home this evening?' he asked suddenly.

'No,' she revealed reluctantly, knowing the reason for the question. But she couldn't tell him an out-and-out lie—he had only to check for himself to know Sally wasn't at home. 'She's gone out for the evening with one of her brother's friends.' She had been pleased for Sally when she had told her she had accepted an invitation from one of her older brother Brian's friends. Sally had insisted it was only a casual date, but at least she had made the effort to get out, proof that she could have a life without the unfaithful Dave.

But Sally having gone out put her in an awkward position. She had used the other girl to avoid asking Luke up to the flat all week, now it looked as if she had to invite him in. 'Would you like to come up for coffee?' she offered.

'Not if that's all you're offering, no,' he told her curtly.

He was making his intention plain before he came up to her flat. If he accepted her invitation he intended making love to her. She either accepted that or left it! But if she left it she might also lose Luke.

'If it takes you this long to decide I won't bother,' he rasped savagely as he stopped the car at her home with a loud screech of the brakes. 'Maybe we *should* put off this visit to my father, until you're more sure of your feelings. The fact that I am taking you to see him is more or less a declaration on my part. I have no intention of telling him in a few weeks' time that it all fell through.'

'You know that won't happen.'

'Do I?' he scorned bitterly. 'I never seem to hear anything but no from you. I'm not used to fighting so hard for what I want, Lori,' he said wearily. 'I'm getting a little tired of it.'

That was what she had thought, what she had dreaded. And yet if she gave in to his demands now she might as well say goodbye to any idea of marriage.

'I think you're right, Luke, we should cancel the visit to see your father,' she told him coolly, opening the car door. 'Until you're more sure of *your* feelings. At the moment they don't appear to be concentrated any higher than your loins!' She slammed the door as she got out, going inside without a second glance.

It must have been at least five suspenseful minutes later before the knock sounded on the door. Lori knew straight away it had to be Luke; she had already checked, surreptitiously, out of the bedroom window, that the Jaguar was still parked outside.

'My feelings may not be concentrated any higher than my loins,' he drawled once she had opened the door, 'which incidentally is a very unladylike thing for you to have said,' he mocked. 'But you have me so frustrated I hardly know what day of the week it is any more. Of course I want you, kitten,' he added in a serious voice. 'I couldn't be in love with you and not want to make love to you. And you've been holding me off all week, denying me even the pleasure of touching you. I need to touch you, Lori,' he said gruffly. 'I need to touch you all the time.'

How it happened she never knew, but she was suddenly lying full length on the sofa with Luke beside her, his jacket and her dress discarded on the way, the buttons on his shirt posing no problem to her questing fingers.

He pushed one cup of her lacy bra aside, capturing the tip of her breast in his mouth, kissing the nipple with a thoroughness that left her gasping, before beginning a slow journey downwards, her flesh seeming to tingle where he touched, his hands continuing the exploration of her breasts.

Of her own volition, it seemed, her hands did some exploring of their own, her lips touching the masculine nipples; she heard him gasp as her mouth continued its downward path of discovery, searching out the pleasure zones of his chest and taut stomach.

Luke's hand slipped beneath the lacy material of her bikini panties, discovering the softness of her thighs, the warmth enveloping her as he caressed her to fever pitch, allowing her no respite from the explosion of pleasure, even when she begged for mercy.

She was lost in a cloud of euphoria as he carried her through to the bedroom, her arms reaching up for him as he laid her down on the narrowness of her single bed.

Instead of joining her he kissed her lightly on the brow, lingeringly on the mouth, gently on her breasts, softly on her thigh, then straightened to look down at her with dark eyes. 'Sweet dreams, my darling,' he said huskily.

'You—you're leaving?' She couldn't believe that the clamouring of her body for possession by his was to be unanswered.

He nodded. 'I have to show you that it's you I love, and not just your body.' He gave a rueful smile as he sat on the side of the bed. 'There's nothing I'd like better than to join my flesh with yours, to lose myself in making love to you. But I have to show you that I don't just want your body, that I want your love more than anything else in the world.' He stood up to button his shirt. 'I love you, Lori, and if this doesn't prove that then I may as well give up.' He was filled with a waiting tension.

She knew the effort it cost him to draw back from

making love to her, could still see the pain in his eyes. 'It proves it,' she acknowledged softly.

His breath caught in his throat at the rose-tinted loveliness of her breasts, and he pulled himself back from her with effort. 'I want your answer now, Lori,' he told her hardly. 'I can't wait any longer. Will you marry me?'

'Yes.' She didn't hesitate, knowing he loved her as deeply as she had wanted him to.

Then why did she have this feeling of depression, a heaviness to her mood, when she should have been silently rejoicing?

Luke closed his eyes, his ragged sigh proof of his relief at her answer, and came down beside her on the bed to give her a lingering kiss on the lips. 'Tell me,' he prompted huskily.

She knew what he wanted her to say, and yet she shied from this deliberate lie, realising for the first time just how innocent in all of this Luke was. She had coldly decided to get to Jacob Randell through his son's love for her, never stopping to think of the consequences to Luke when she callously destroyed that love.

Luke had proved he wasn't a man who loved easily, and the fact that he had admitted to loving her so deeply from the beginning meant that he was going to be devastated when she ended it for him. Why hadn't she thought of that before she entered into this? Because she hadn't thought of Luke at all then, hadn't cared what happened to him in her revenge on his father!

But she cared now. She cared more than she had realised! 'I love you,' she told him, and knew it was the truth.

She had fallen in love with Luke without even

knowing she had; she loved the son of the man she had hated most of her life. And Luke wasn't a man who would forgive easily. When he knew the truth he would want to destroy her as ruthlessly as she had wanted to destroy his father.

'I love you, Luke!' she choked, raising her arms to pull him down to her, tears in her eyes slowly cascading down her cheeks as she returned the warmth of his kiss.

What could she do? How could she stop her plans for revenge backfiring on her in the cruellest way possible?

CHAPTER TEN

LORI was very subdued on the journey to Luke's father's the next day, having spent a sleepless night.

Luke had left shortly after she had told him she loved him, and when Sally arrived home half an hour later Lori was aware that it was her turn to pretend to be asleep, avoiding all personal questions.

And all the time the tears had streamed down her cheeks in her silent misery. When it had happened, *how* it had happened, she just didn't know; all she knew was that when Luke went out of her life, as inevitably he would, she would want to die.

It was as if she had been caught up in one of those terrible dreams she had trouble escaping from the last few weeks. But the dream, or nightmare, was over now, and she had been left with only the stark reality of her love for Luke.

She loved him, loved everything about him, the thick darkness of his hair with the distinguishing grey streaks at his temples, the warm grey of his eyes when he looked at her, the hook of his nose, the indulgent curve of his mouth, and the hard beauty of his body. She loved the quickness of his mind, his strength, his air of command. She just loved the man himself, knew that her love equalled the intensity of his.

And she was caught in the vortex of revenge, revenge of her own making, a revenge that would ultimately destroy all Luke's love for her. There was no way she could put a stop to this mad spiralling towards the end of the plan, the ultimate bitter end was out of her hands now. And it would be bitter; this wonderful man at her side had already told her his opinion of Lorraine Chisholm by his reaction to Nigel's broken engagement. Once he knew that *she* was Lorraine Chisholm he would never forgive her. She had no doubt that Luke's love was genuine enough now, but once he knew who she was ... She shivered with apprehension.

'Anything wrong, darling?' Luke glanced at her anxiously, sensing her shiver. 'I'm sorry if I've given you the wrong impression,' he smiled. 'My father isn't exactly an ogre. We don't get on, but I'm sure he'll be charming to you,' his mouth twisted. 'He has an eye for a beautiful woman.'

Lori chewed worriedly on her bottom lip. It was that perception of Jacob Randell's that she feared. Twelve years had passed, twelve long years for her, and during that time she had grown from a confused young girl to a confident woman, and yet basically her appearance was the same. She might have matured, slimmed down, but she still had a cloud of red-gold hair, sparkling brown eyes, refined features.

'Don't worry, kitten,' Luke put out a hand to clasp hers, 'I'll be by your side.'

She was glad of that when she met Jacob Randell!

The house Luke parked the Jaguar outside was situated about fifty miles from London in a sleepy little village in Surrey; the house was more like a large cottage, painted white to fit in with the other houses in the village.

Luke got out of the car to come round and open Lori's door for her. 'Not exactly what you would expect of Jacob P. Randell, is it?' he scorned.

It certainly wasn't. But if the house came as a surprise to her, Jacob Randell was even more of one. He was in a wheelchair!

The maid took them out to the lawned garden at the back of the house, where in a wheelchair beneath the big sunshade sat an elderly man, his iron-grey hair now snowy white, the piercing eyes that had once seemed to see into a person's very soul now dulled with age.

All Lori could feel as she looked down at this rather sad old man was pity, making a mockery of her vengeful plans for retribution for her parents and her own unhappiness.

'I hope you'll excuse my not getting up.' His voice was as strong as ever, deep and commanding. 'But as you can see, I'm not able to.' He smiled to take the sharpness out of his words.

'No,' she said without sympathy, sensing a self-pity she wouldn't have believed possible in such a compelling man. What was the saying, 'The bigger you are the harder you fall'? Jacob Randell had certainly fallen! She looked about her appreciatively. 'You have a lovely home, Mr Randell.'

'Yes,' he sighed, unimpressed, and turned to his son. 'So, Luke, this is the young lady you wanted me to meet.'

Lori looked up at Luke, a Luke she had never seen before. He was coldly removed, his eyes icy as he looked down at his father, giving absolutely nothing away of his thoughts from his expression.

'Yes, this is Lori.' His arm moved about her waist in a possessive gesture. 'My fiancée.'

'Indeed?' Silver-coloured eyes widened as Jacob Randell looked at Lori with new eyes.

She tensed under that sharp appraisal. Did he recognise her as the daughter of Michael Chisholm, *could* he recognise her beneath the sophisticated veneer of Lori Parker? She wasn't sure she could cope with the scene such a revelation would cause, and she moved instinctively against Luke's side, feeling his arm tighten about her waist as he looked down at her anxiously.

'Your taste, as usual, is impeccable, Luke,' his father drawled. 'Could you go and ask Mrs James to serve tea?' He looked up challengingly at the younger man.

Luke seemed to hesitate; he nodded slowly and reluctantly, giving Lori a regretful shrug before striding into the house to speak to the housekeeper.

'Sit down, my dear.'

She turned nervously to Jacob Randell, the longing still in her eyes from where she had watched Luke leave, and sat down abruptly on one of the garden chairs, perching on its edge.

'I'm not that frightening, am I, Lori?' Jacob Randell mocked her nervousness.

She moistened her suddenly dry lips. 'I—What do you mean?'

'You've gone quite white,' he smiled enquiringly.

That smile—how well she remembered that smile! It was like a lure for unsuspecting innocents.

'It's Lori, isn't it?' He raised white brows, a thin man, his imposing height lost in the wheelchair, his lean face lined with age, bitter humour in his eyes. 'Or is that just my son's pet name for you?'

'No. No!' she said more strongly as her voice came out as a husky squeak. 'My name is Lori.'

'Unusual,' he said softly.

Delicate colour winged her cheeks, and she looked at him worriedly, unconsciously pleating the pretty brown and cream cotton skirt she wore with a brown tee-shirt. 'Yes,' she said huskily.

'So you intend marrying my son?'

'Yes,' she nodded, knowing she could never be Luke's wife.

'When is the wedding to be?' His eyes were narrowed.

'We—er—we haven't decided on a date yet,' she blushed.

'No?'

'We only became engaged yesterday.' She was becoming agitated.

Jacob Randell smiled again. 'My son doesn't usually waste any time once he's decided to do something.'

There was no answer she could make to that, knowing first-hand of Luke's haste she had been the object of his impatience since she had first met him, when she had had no intention of either loving him or marrying him. Now she loved him too much, and she could never marry him.

'Your fiancée doesn't seem too sure of me,' Jacob Randell looked up to drawl.

Relief flooded Lori's face as she saw Luke had rejoined them. She smiled reassuringly as he raised his dark brows in questioning anxiety, loving the way his hair curled darkly over the collar of the light grey shirt he wore with black trousers, seeing him move with all the forceful elegance his father had once possessed.

He sat down beside her and took her hand in his, entwining his fingers with hers. 'My father hasn't been—teasing you, has he?' he asked tautly, an underlying steel to his voice.

'Er——'

'When have you ever known me to tease, Luke?' his father mocked his tension.

'Never,' his son rasped. 'Lori?' he prompted hardly.

She frowned, not wanting to be the cause of an argument between these two men—there seemed to be enough friction between them already! 'Your father and I were just talking,' she assured him lightly.

'I was asking Lori when the wedding is going to be,' his father told him.

Cool grey eyes were turned on the older man. 'I'll let you know when Lori and I have decided on the date,' Luke rasped. 'You'll want to be there?'

'Of course,' his father nodded tautly.

'Of course,' Luke drawled derisively.

The antagonism between the two men seemed to lessen slightly as tea was served by a small rounded woman who retreated back to the house as soon as she had put the tray down on the table.

'I see you're still terrifying the life out of Mrs James,' Luke taunted as Lori poured the tea.

'She stills runs like a frightened rabbit, if that's what you mean,' his father chuckled his enjoyment of such sport.

Their tea on the lawn must have looked so pleasant to an outsider, only Lori seemed aware of the undercurrents between father and son, of her own nervousness of the time-bombs that existed within each of them waiting to go off.

She felt immense relief when Luke suggested they leave an hour later, standing up immediately.

'Your future bride seems anxious to leave,' Jacob mused, looking up at her with mocking eyes, cruelty in their depths. 'I think she finds us a little overwhelming together.'

'Most people do,' Luke snapped. 'I know Mother always did.'

His father's expression became harsh. 'Let's not bring your mother into this.'

'No,' Luke rasped agreement, 'let's not. I'll let you know about the wedding.'

'It was nice meeting you, Lori,' Jacob told her smoothly, controlling the anger that had made him flare up at Luke seconds earlier.

Luke seemed disinclined to talk for the first ten miles

of their journey back to London, and Lori was lost in her own thoughts. She had been dreading that meeting with Jacob Randell, and it had turned out to be as traumatic as she had imagined.

Oh, she no longer feared the omnipotent Jacob P. Randell, rather she pitied him. He was a bitter old man who was living out his life confined to a wheelchair, without the love of his only child, without the love of anyone. All he had left were his memories of a past career—and a loneliness that had aged him prematurely.

'I had no idea your father was in a wheelchair.' She turned to Luke with a frown.

'He doesn't like to advertise the fact, and to be honest I hardly notice it,' he said harshly. 'It doesn't seem to have made any difference to his effectiveness. He still has the tongue of a viper!'

'How did it happen?' Her voice was husky.

'A back injury in a car accident. My mother was killed in the same accident,' Luke added hardly.

'I'm sorry.'

'Yes, so am I. *He* should have been the one that died. God, I'm sorry!' he groaned as he heard her shocked gasp. 'Visiting my father is guaranteed to put me in a foul temper. As you probably gathered, there's no love lost between us.'

'Yes,' she nodded.

He drew in a deep, calming breath. 'Satisfied now that you've met him?'

'Oh, Luke!' she choked, clasping his arm. 'I wish——'

'I know.' His fingers moved to entwine with hers.

If only he did, if only he could understand the bitterness that she had known for so long, and which had now faded with her love for him. She could so easily have lived with that hatred all her life and ended up as old and embittered as Jacob Randell himself. She shivered at the thought of that; she knew that Jacob Randell's son had been the one, ironically, to save her from such fate. She might lose Luke in the end, but she would never again be that woman full of hatred, afraid to love.

'Did it put you off me?' Luke asked in a lighter tone.

'No,' she smiled at him. 'You aren't your father.' And she had realised that too late, *too late* . . .!

'Shall we go and get your ring tomorrow?'

'Tomorrow?' She swallowed hard.

'There's no reason to wait,' he shrugged. 'Poor Paul and Nikki have some shocks in store for them when they get back today—Claude in hospital, and now our engagement.'

'Could we—could we keep it to ourselves for a while?' Lori looked at him appealingly.

He frowned. 'Why?'

'Because—well, because we haven't known each other very long,' she smiled jerkily. 'I thought perhaps we could——'

'I want everyone to know you belong to me. One person in particular,' he added grimly.

She knew instantly who he meant. 'Jonathan,' she said slowly. 'But you know he means nothing to me, Luke,' she frowned.

'I won't be sure of that until you're mine, until I've banished every other man from your heart and your body! And I will banish them, Lori,' he rasped, 'if it takes me our lifetime together.'

'Luke,' she moistened her lips with the tip of her tongue, swallowing hard, 'there are no other men, there never were, not in my heart, and not—not in my body.' She knew now that she couldn't have loved Nigel, had known none of this fevered longing with him, hadn't felt one tenth of the despair at losing him that she felt just at the thought of never seeing Luke again. 'I—I lied to you about that,' she blushed.

'Why?' he asked gruffly.

'Because I—I——'

'Because I was arrogant,' he said ruefully. 'But maybe you shouldn't have told me the truth, kitten,' he grimaced.

Her eyes widened. 'Why not?'

He glanced at her, a fire burning in the depths of his eyes. 'Because I intended taking you home with me and showing you exactly how much I love you. Now I think we'd better wait.'

'No!' Colour flooded her cheeks at his surprised expression. 'No, Luke,' she repeated calmly. 'I'd like to come home with you.' Her tone was pleading.

His breath caught in his throat. 'You're sure?' A fierce light gleamed in his eyes.

'Very sure,' she nodded eagerly, wondering if she could possibly be the same woman who had so coldly, calculatedly, decided Luke should fall deeply in love with her. Instead she was the one who was a slave to that love.

Luke put his foot down on the accelerator. 'Let's hope I don't get booked for speeding,' he muttered as he liberally broke the speed limits all the way back to London.

Lori laughed happily at his side, her hand touching his arm, her eyes glowing with a recklessness she had never known before. She felt no sense of nervousness, not even when they entered his totally male-orientated apartment. The very size of it was enough to overwhelm her; it was big enough to have fitted the tiny flat she shared with Sally inside at least four times.

But she didn't care about that; she cared only for the promise in Luke's eyes, the deep desire as he looked down at her in the darkness, framing her face with his hands, kissing each eyelid, the tip of her nose, and finally—achingly, her mouth, seeming to draw the very soul from the depths of her body.

She stood on tiptoe to open her mouth to his, her fingers curled into the hair at his nape, her breasts pressed against the hardness of his chest, and he shuddered against her.

As Lori winced Luke raised his head with a groan, seeing how reddened her chin had become. 'I need a shave,' he realised ruefully. 'Or I'll mark you all over this beautiful body of yours.' He took her hand in his to lead her through to his bedroom, closing the door on the outside world, the moonlight streaming through the huge window their only form of light. 'Two minutes,' he promised, 'then we'll have all night.'

He left the door to the adjoining bathroom open, and Lori stood in the darkness watching him as he stripped off the shirt, his torso strong and powerful, before deftly shaving the growth of beard from his face.

A huge shower gleamed invitingly behind him, and she suddenly had the urge to stand beneath the cleansing spray, to wash all the emotions of the day from her body before she and Luke began their discovery of the night.

It took her only a matter of seconds to strip the clothes from her body, knowing as she gently pushed the bathroom door open wider that she had nothing to be ashamed of, sure of it as Luke gasped at the surge of desire that flooded his body.

Lori smiled a woman's secret smile of satisfaction at his reaction to her nakedness, and turned on the shower tap before holding out her hand to him. 'Come and join me.' She stepped beneath the heated water.

Luke stepped beneath the spray fully clothed, his gaze fixed on the parted invitation of her lips, his trousers plastered to him in a matter of seconds, his hair ebony as he lowered his head to part her lips further with the invasion of his mouth.

'Take off the rest of your clothes,' she encouraged shakily as he kissed each aching nipple, driving her insane with the butterfly caresses of his mouth against her hardened flesh.

'Take them off for me,' he groaned his encouragement. 'Make love to me, kitten.'

She had never undressed a man before, kissing the broadness of his back and chest before unzipping his trousers with trembling hands, removing the black underpants that remained his only article of clothing, his skin gleaming deeply gold as he stood naked in front of her. He was beautiful, so beautiful he made her tremble in anticipation.

'Take me, Luke,' she begged. 'Take me now!' She was too aroused to wait any longer, the wildfire excitement burning through her veins was crying out for his thrusting possession.

'Darling——?'

'Now!' She curved herself against him, her arms about his neck as she felt him probing her parted thighs. She was the one to make the final move that made her one with him, her cry lost in the warm vortex of his mouth, her spiralling to the floor prevented by Luke's arms like steel bands about her body. 'Oh, Luke ...!' she groaned as he began to move inside her, reaching deep within her, touching each nerve-ending, each particle of her body, each surge of his possession building up the pressure of ever-increasing pleasure, a pleasure she knew he intended her to reach before he took his own shuddering desire.

They reached the very pinnacle of that passion in unison. Luke's heart-felt groan of intense pleasure was lost against her throat as she could only gasp at the fiery ecstasy that had taken her completely by surprise.

Her next gasp was one of shock as Luke turned the water to cold, holding her squirming body in his arms as the freezing cold water washed over them both. 'Luke, no——!' Tears shone in her eyes at this cruelty. 'Luke . . .?' she groaned, beginning to shiver, her body tinglingly alive, the water now feeling like tiny pinpricks on her cooled flesh.

He carried her to his bed, laying her beneath the covers, instantly joining her, clinging to her damply, then he began to make love to her all over again, the coldness of the water having heightened her senses so that each caress seemed to burn, and their coming together was as fevered as before.

'You devil!' she groaned.

'Witch!' Luke ruefully rubbed the spot on his shoulder where her teeth had bitten into him. 'I'll probably bear the scars of your passion for life!'

'So will I.' Her tone didn't match his lighthearted one, her eyes were already taking on a haunted look. She belonged body and soul to Luke now, and soon he wouldn't want her! She turned to him once again, a glorious desperation in the heat of her mouth on his. 'Love me again, Luke,' she pleaded. 'Please love me again!'

He laughed softly, exultantly. 'If you're this demanding when we're married I'll never get to work, and if I do I'll be too tired to do anything!' His eyes gleamed down at her, gently teasing. 'Still, who's worried about work?' he dismissed wolfishly, his mouth claiming hers once again.

It was after eight when Luke drove her home the next

morning, telling her he would wait for her while she
changed for work. Lori insisted he go on alone,
knowing she owed Sally some explanation for last
night, and that it would be better made alone.

'Meet another fool,' she told the other girl ruefully
when she entered the flat to find her friend in the
kitchen eating breakfast.

'Not the same at all.' Sally stood up. 'Luke happens
to love you, he has from the start—anyone can see that.
Like some toast?' she offered with a smile.

Lori felt none of the embarrassment in front of her
friend that she had been expecting, and she knew it was
mainly due to Sally's lack of inquisitiveness. 'No,
thanks.' She went to the bedroom to discard the tee-
shirt and skirt she had worn yesterday. 'I've already
eaten.' Breakfast had been a hilarious affair, so much so
that Luke had taken her back to bed, all the laughter
suddenly fading, leaving the blazing desire that nothing
seemed to extinguish.

Sally nodded, standing in the doorway as Lori
donned one of the smart suits and feminine blouses she
wore to work. 'How did the meeting with his father go?'
she asked interestedly. 'Is he as formidable as they say?'

'No,' Lori answered truthfully, without any real need
for thought. 'He's just a rather sad old man,' she
dismissed. 'How did your date with Gary go on
Saturday?' The two of them had had little opportunity
to talk since then.

Sally shrugged. 'Okay. I went out with him for the
day yesterday too. I don't think he's going to be the
grand passion of my life, but he's nice. By the way, you
had a visitor yesterday.'

'I did?' Lori was busy looking in the wardrobe for the
matching black shoe to the one she held in her hand.

'Mm,' Sally frowned.

'Who was it?' She had found the shoe, and slipped them both on to her narrow feet.

'He didn't say,' Sally shrugged.

'He?' Lori's interest sharpened.

'Yes,' Sally nodded. 'He just asked for you, and when I told him you weren't here he said he would be in touch.'

'Not when Luke's around, I hope,' Lori smiled. 'He tends to be rather—possessive.' She still bore the bruises from his reaction to Jonathan kissing her.

'I've noticed!' her friend grimaced.

Lori looked at her wrist-watch. 'We'd better be going, or we'll be late. Nikki and Paul come back today,' she realised with a smile.

'Nikki couldn't look any happier than you do today. You look beautiful, Lori,' Sally told her huskily.

'Thank you,' she blushed, knowing her night in Luke's arms had given her an ecstatic glow.

Luke's door was closed when she entered her own office, and she knew it was just as well. This brief respite from the flaring passion in his eyes would enable her to at least open the mail, knowing she wouldn't be able to work once he was close to her, looking at her, touching her.

Last night had been the most beautiful experience of her life, even more so when she had woken to find herself held tightly in Luke's arms. Then he had kissed her with gentle adoration, told her how much he loved and needed her, demanding that she move in with him until they could be married at the end of the week. As she had known there wouldn't be a wedding she had agreed; she was going to take all the happiness she could with him before her bubble of happiness burst for ever.

The door to Luke's office opened, and she looked up

with a loving smile, a smile that froze on her lips as she recognised the man who stood there. Nigel Phillips. And he had been in to see Luke!

What could he have said to him? What had he told him? She knew the answer to that. Her happiness had been taken from her much quicker than she had anticipated.

CHAPTER ELEVEN

NIGEL closed the door as he came further into her office, barely having changed at all. His blond hair was kept short, he was still tall and slim, only the few lines evident about his eyes telling her of the passing of five years.

She looked at him now with new eyes, wondering how she could ever have loved him enough to begin this strange revenge on Luke. Oh, Nigel was handsome enough, and yet there was an air of condescension about him, superciliousness that made her wonder how he had ever dared defy his father enough to even contemplate marrying her.

Next to Luke's strength and determination to succeed Nigel paled to nothingness, and Lori looked at him coolly as he walked over to her desk. 'Nigel,' she nodded distantly.

'Lori,' his tone was curt. 'You know why I'm here?'

Her mouth twisted, although she refused to let him see the pain in her shadowed brown eyes. 'It isn't difficult to guess.' And it wasn't. Nigel felt she had humiliated him five years ago, and he wasn't a man who forgot easily either.

'No,' he snapped, his gaze insolent as it swept over her slender curves. 'You're more beautiful than ever,' he rasped, as if that knowledge angered him.

Her eyes widened as she saw an emotion she barely recognised flicker briefly in his eyes. Love. She had seen love gleam there for a few brief seconds. And yet he had come here today to deliberately destroy her life once again.

'Did you call on me yesterday?' she asked woodenly.

'Yes,' he nodded, the dark suit fitting him wonderfully, emphasising the width and power of his shoulders, the lean length of his legs. 'You were out with Randell, according to your flatmate,' he added harshly. 'Randell, Lori?' he scorned. 'I would have thought you would have chosen anyone but him! You once made your feelings about his father perfectly clear.'

Dull colour ebbed into her cheeks as she remembered the conversation. It was part of her dream, it always preceded the scene where Nigel walked out of her life, when she had lost control and told Nigel and his father that Jacob Randell had been wrong about her father, that she hated him, had always hated him.

'Now it appears you're in love with his son,' Nigel scorned. 'I find that very hard to believe. And so did he!'

Lori paled as rapidly as she had blushed. 'What did you tell him?'

'Just the truth,' Nigel drawled, sitting on the edge of her desk. 'I told him how you had always vowed vengeance on his father.'

'And he—he believed you?' She could hear the faint murmur of Luke's voice from the inner office as he spoke to someone on the telephone. Probably having her removed from the practice!

'Of course,' Nigel confirmed contemptuously. 'It's the truth, isn't it?'

'Yes,' she choked. 'Margot recognised me, of course,' she said in a pained voice.

'Eventually,' Nigel nodded. 'She told me about you when I returned from my honeymoon over the weekend.'

'Your wife is very beautiful,' she told him dully, still

conscious of Luke talking on the telephone in the other room.

'Yes,' Nigel acknowledged abruptly. 'Her father is Lord Maughan.'

'So I read,' Lori nodded absently, wondering what Luke was thinking now, why he hadn't thundered out here and demanded an explanation, that would have been more his style than this waiting game. But the door between the two offices remained firmly closed.

'He's a judge, you know,' Nigel added smugly.

No, she hadn't known, but it followed that he would have married a woman who could bring him more than herself. Lori knew she must have been an unexpected weakness on his part. Nigel was an ambitious man, and having a judge as his father-in-law would be a tremendous boost to his career. He might even be planning to advance his career in that direction when he was older.

'How nice for you,' she taunted dryly.

He nodded, not even noticing her sarcasm. 'Caroline is a very suitable wife.'

'I'm glad,' she said stiffly.

'Are you?' He looked at her coldly. 'You did your best to ruin my life five years ago.'

'And now you've deliberately ruined mine!'

'Yes.' Nigel stood up, straightening his cuff. 'Poetic justice, don't you think?'

She flushed, swallowing hard. 'You've found happiness now.'

'Yes,' he bent down to look her fully in the face, only inches away from her, 'but you don't know how desperately I wish it could have been you.' His face was shadowed. 'I loved you, Lori, more that I've ever loved anyone—including Caroline. Maybe now that I'm married and you're free of Randell——'

'Yes?' she demanded tautly, hardly able to believe what she was hearing. She couldn't believe she was to suffer this further humiliation on top of her other pain.

'There's no reason why you and I shouldn't—meet,' Nigel said softly. 'When it's mutually convenient, of course.'

She closed her eyes, a red tide of anger passing in front of her. 'And if it's never—convenient?' she asked through gritted teeth.

'Why wouldn't it be?' he taunted. 'You and Randell have been lovers. I know damn well you have been,' he rasped viciously, 'by the way he reacted when I told him who you are. But I already know all there is to know about you, and I still want you.'

Lori stood up, shaking with anger. 'Get out of here,' she told him coldly. 'How I could ever have imagined myself in love with you I'll never know! You're disgusting and obnoxious! Now get out. You've done all you've set out to do, caused enough harm for one day!'

His eyes widened incredulously. 'You've actually *fallen in love* with Randell!'

'Yes!'

'My God!' He gave a contemptuous laugh, and was still laughing as he walked to the door. 'Poor Lori,' he taunted, leaving quietly.

Poor Lori, indeed. There was still no movement from Luke's office, although the telephone conversation seemed to have stopped now, the silence was ominous. Lori longed to go and knock on the door, but she feared the outcome.

'Is it all right if I come in?' Nikki put her head around the side of the door, a glowingly happy Nikki; her first few weeks of marriage had obviously been a success. She came right into the room, her eyes lightly teasing. 'Only I've heard rumours that it isn't always safe to walk into a room when you and Luke are alone together!'

Lori's smile was brittle; she was not willing to upset Nikki when she looked so ecstatically happy. 'Really? And who told you that?'

'Claude,' Nikki giggled, sobering suddenly. 'We went to see him yesterday. He looks well, better than I've seen him for months.'

'Yes,' Lori nodded.

'Of course Paul's angry because he wasn't told, but I can only admire Claude for what he did.' Nikki sat down. 'Paul's talking to Luke on the telephone now.'

Lori knew that he wasn't, that the conversation had finished minutes ago. And still Luke remained in his office. What was he *doing*?

'How do you like your new boss?' Nikki teased once again.

'I—like him,' Lori admitted huskily.

'Claude seemed to think you more than liked him.' Nikki looked at her questioningly.

Her smile was bright. 'I don't think so,' she shook her head. 'In fact, he would prefer it if you worked for him.'

'He would?' Nikki sounded puzzled.

'Yes. Would you mind?'

The other girl shrugged. 'Not really. Although it's up to Paul. I——'

The inner office door opened, and Luke at last emerged, a Luke totally unrecognisable as the man in whose arms she had woken this morning. His face was pale, his eyes glacial, there was an unapproachable hardness to his whole body. He returned Nikki's cheerful greeting with an abruptness that had her leaving within seconds.

Lori felt compelled to say something, to at least speak. 'Luke, I——'

'Would you come in here?' He stepped back to open the door for her.

'Oh, Luke——'

'Could you wait until we're in my office,' he said stonily.

She meekly walked past him, sitting down as he began to pace the room, sensing his gaze on her often as she looked down at her clasped hands in her lap, knowing that if they were unclasped they would be trembling uncontrollably.

'It's too much to hope that it isn't the truth?' his voice rasped into the uncomfortably silence.

'Yes——' her voice broke.

'Why the hell didn't you tell me? No, let me guess,' he dismissed coldly. 'If I'd known who you were you couldn't even have begun your revenge. Could you?' he bit out harshly.

'No.' Lori still looked down at her hands.

'So you don't deny that you went out with me with revenge in mind?'

'No. But——'

'And last night?' he bit out savagely. 'Was that out of revenge too?'

Now she did look up at him, her eyes darkened with pain. 'No!' Her denial was a plea.

'No?' His eyes were like chips of ice, all love gone from the harshness of his granite-like features. 'Wasn't that to ensure that when you twisted the knife of your identity in my guts I knew the full agony of losing you?'

'No——'

'Well, I know the full agony, Lori,' he rasped. 'Last night I thought I held the woman I loved in my arms, the woman I thought loved me in return, and instead you were willing to go that far, to give me your virginity, so that my pain should be tenfold.' The contempt shone in his eyes. 'Tell me, when was the revelation of your being Michael Chisholm's daughter going to come out, before or after I married you?'

'After. But——'

'Of course, after,' his tone was self-derisive. 'Michael Chisholm's daughter as *my* wife!'

Lori stood up agitatedly, knowing Luke had a right to be angry, that she had no real way of vindicating herself. All that he had said so far was true . . .

'What was Nigel Phillips talking to you about just now?' Luke demanded sharply. 'Oh yes, I could hear the two of you,' he mocked her gasp of surprise.

Of course he could. If she could hear him on the telephone then he had to know of her conversation with Nigel. Her head went back. 'He offered me an affair,' she told him almost defiantly.

Luke's eyes narrowed to icy slits. 'And did you accept?'

'Of course not!'

'Why not?' he growled fiercely. 'He's the reason for all this, isn't he? Not your father at all, but Nigel Phillips.'

She avoided the demand of his eyes. 'I don't know what you mean.'

'When he came in here and told me you were Lorraine Chisholm, that you'd once sworn revenge on my father, my first reaction was to go into your office and shake the hell out of you.' His hands clenched and unclenched, as if he would still like to do that. 'But I gave myself time to think, to reflect. You suddenly changed towards me the weekend after Nigel was married. I knew all about your broken engagement to him five years ago—at least, I knew of Lorraine Chisholm's broken engagement to him. In fact, it was because of that that I refused to go to his wedding this time.'

'I—I don't understand,' Lori frowned.

'No, you wouldn't,' his mouth twisted. 'But then, despite spending the night with me, you don't appear to know me very well, do you? Do you think I approve of what my father did to yours?' he rasped. 'That I could live with the way he mentally persecuted a man so that the man took his own life? Well, I couldn't!' He looked down at her fiercely. 'I hated the way he handled your father's case, despised him for the mental anguish he caused him, whether he was guilty or not, hated him when your father, through sheer desperation, committed suicide.'

Lori had flinched as he taunted her about the night she had spent with him, going deathly pale as he revealed his feelings about the way her father had been pushed into committing suicide. She had had so many hints as to the contempt Luke felt for his father—the way he had suddenly left England all those years ago, the friction, the dislike almost, between him and his father, Claude's mention of the clash of personalities between them, the fact that there had never been any possibility of Luke working with his father. It had all been there for her to see, and in her blindness for revenge she had missed it all!

'I hated what he did to your mother, to you,' Luke continued in a steely voice. 'I even tried to find your mother afterwards—God knows what I thought I could do,' he derided harshly. 'Said how sorry I was, at the very least. Although I'm sure that wouldn't have helped your mother; nothing could at a time like that.' He drew in a ragged breath. 'I had no idea of the deep psychological effect it would have on you, of the lengths you would go to to get your revenge. Do you still love Nigel, is that it?' he asked coldly.

'I love you,' she told him brokenly, shocked to the core by all that he had told her. Not that she doubted a word of it, she knew him well enough now to know that this was exactly the way he would have reacted to his father's public cruelty to another man.

'Spare me that,' he dismissed harshly.

'It's the truth——'

'I can't accept that,' he shook his head. 'And even if I could, it would never work between us now. Every time we argued—and we would argue a lot,' he added dryly, 'you would remember what my father did to yours. I couldn't live with that.'

'I wouldn't ask any more than to be with you!' Tears glistened in her eyes. 'You could tell me to leave any time you wanted to.'

His expression was closed, the dullness of his eyes telling her nothing of his reaction to her impassioned plea. 'I'm telling you to leave now,' he said softly, and turned away, his shoulders hunched as he thrust his hands into his trousers pockets. 'I've already arranged with Paul to have Nikki as my secretary as from this morning. He should be telling her of the change now.'

'If you would rather I just left immediately——'

'No,' he mocked. 'Claude still isn't very strong, and knowing that his favourite secretary has walked out could cause a setback. I'd like you to stay until Claude is completely recovered.'

'And then leave?' Lori stared at his rigid back.

'Yes,' he nodded coldly. 'And then leave.'

She turned with a choked sob and ran from the room.

What followed had to be the worst week of her life, a time when she reached her lowest ebb. If she had thought herself desolate when she lost Nigel she now knew what true desolation was.

Luke was only an arrogant figure walking about the building to her, never acknowledging that he ever noticed her, let alone the open longing in her eyes as she gazed after him. And if her days were spent trying just to catch a glimpse of him, her nights were spent aching for him, the awakening of her body making her groan with unfulfilment. If Sally noticed her pacing up and down the lounge during the night-time hours then she gave no indication of it, although she did encourage Lori to go out with her on a couple of occasions.

When she lunched with Nikki she heard all about Luke's foul moods, and while she had found him to be an exacting employer, he hadn't really been a bad-tempered one. They were both suffering because of the situation she had created, with no possible solution to the fact that they seemed to love each other but couldn't be together.

'What on earth is the matter with you?' her aunt frowned as Lori arrived for her visit on Sunday. 'You look terrible!'

'I knew I came to see you for a reason,' Lori said with forced lightness. 'It's to make me feel good!' she grimaced.

'No need for sarcasm, young lady.' Aunt Jessie looked disapprovingly over her glasses. 'You aren't too big to smack, you know. Now where's Luke?'

Straight for the jugular, that was Aunt Jessie! 'I'm not seeing him any more,' Lori answered with equal bluntness.

'Why not?'

'Because I'm not,' she shrugged.

Her aunt frowned. 'I have a terrible thought running through my mind,' she groaned. 'Didn't he know you were Michael's daughter?'

'You mean you know who Luke is?' Lori gasped, taut with surprise.

'Of course I know,' her aunt told her waspishly. 'I'm not senile, girl! I knew as soon as I heard his surname. I thought you'd decided to be sensible about the Randells—but I have a feeling you haven't,' she sighed.

'No,' Lori confirmed huskily.

'You're such a silly girl, Lorraine,' Aunt Jessie shook her head. 'The past is the past, and should remain that way. You love him, don't you?'

'Yes.'

'And he's in love with you too. So why can't you both forget the past?'

'I have—he can't. Oh, not because he blames me in any way for what Dad did——'

'Do you realise,' her aunt interrupted gently, 'that this is the first time you've ever admitted that your father could have been guilty?'

Lori nodded. 'But he wasn't.'

'Yes,' Aunt Jessie said softly, 'he was.'

Lori blinked dazedly, sure that she had misheard. 'Aunt Jessie . . .?'

The old lady sighed. 'I really can't go on deceiving you any longer, Lorraine, you have to know the truth. I told Sandra she should have told you, but she wouldn't have it.'

'Have what?' Her mouth suddenly felt dry.

'Your father—my nephew—was guilty of everything Luke's father accused him of. He killed himself because Jacob Randell would have been bringing evidence into the case the next day that would have blackened your father for ever. Your father's mistress was going to testify against him.'

Lori swallowed hard, turning very pale. 'M-mistress?'

'She was a woman your father had known for almost

two years,' her aunt nodded. 'The money he had stolen was going to set them up for life once he had left your mother and you.'

'But I—The letter! He always claimed he was innocent!' Lori shook her head disbelievingly.

'There was no letter, Lorraine,' her aunt told her. 'At least, not one your father ever wrote.'

'Mummy——'

'—Wrote it,' Aunt Jessie confirmed.

'But why?' she cried her puzzlement. 'Why lie to me?'

'You were twelve years old, had already been hurt enough, and your mother didn't want you to know about the man your father had really been, the real reason he had killed himself. I can see now why she didn't,' her aunt sighed wearily. 'I haven't liked doing it myself. But it had to be done,' she added briskly.

'But Mummy—she seemed to lose all will to live after Daddy died.'

'She stood by him all during the trial, believed in his innocence. And then she found out about his mistress, his plans to leave her. It broke her spirit, Lorraine, left her no reason to carry on, not even for you. I've let you continue to believe this nonsense about your father's innocence for too long. I didn't even feel regret when that young Judas walked out on you when he learnt the truth—he was too weak for you. But Luke is a good man, and I won't stand by and see you lose him for the same reason.'

'But my knowing the truth makes no difference,' Lori groaned. 'Can't you see that, Aunt Jessie? It just proves that Luke's father was right all the time!'

'And that it's time Luke did some forgiving of his own. Oh yes,' her aunt nodded at her surprised look, 'I know about the bad feeling between him and his father. He told me himself that he isn't close to his father, although not the reason for it, and not who his father was. But just because I've put myself in this home it doesn't mean I don't know what's going on in the rest of the world, or that I can't see what has to be done to right a wrong. And this is wrong, Lorraine. Now I've told you the truth, and I want you to go to Luke and tell it to him.'

'Aunt Jessie,' Lori said slowly, dazedly, 'if Jacob Randell had the evidence all the time that my father was guilty, if he knew about this—this other woman, and the money, why didn't he just say so and exonerate himself with Luke?'

'I think you would have to ask Mr Randell that.'

Ask Jacob Randell? No, she couldn't do that, couldn't face that mockingly cruel man with the fact that she was Lorraine Chisholm.

And yet two hours later she found herself driving to his house, not allowing herself the luxury of thought, just driving, hoping that when she got there he would be out. He wasn't.

'Tell him Miss Chisholm would like to see him,' she asked the housekeeper after being told Mr Randell was indeed at home. 'Miss Lorraine Chisholm.'

She had no idea what she was going to say to Jacob Randell when she saw him, she only knew she had to start off with no deception between them.

She couldn't pretend not to be hurt and bewildered by the man her father had really been, having idolised him for so many years, but it had been so much more unbearable for her mother, living with the lie of her husband's innocence, knowing how he had deceived and hurt her, that he had intended leaving her.

'Would you like to go in, Miss Chisholm?'

She looked up at the smiling housekeeper and nodded abruptly. 'Thank you.'

Jacob Randell sat in the drawing room, looking out of the window, the English summer proving as unpredictable as ever, a light rain falling outside. He turned his chair as he heard her approach, a smile of welcome on his lips. 'Lori!' he greeted warmly. 'Luke isn't with you?'

'No, I'm alone.' She frowned. 'You don't seem surprised to see me.'

His white brows rose. 'Miss Chisholm?' he guessed with a smile. 'No, I knew who you were the moment we met. I remember you and your mother very well—I'm sorry about her death, by the way. But I knew instantly who you were—you haven't changed that much in twelve years, Lori,' he lightly mocked. 'Now what can I do for you?'

'Help me,' she groaned, and sat down, pleading aid from a man she had thought she would never want to talk to, let alone ask help of. 'Why didn't you ever tell the truth about my father?'

For a moment he seemed to hesitate, and then he sighed. 'Hadn't I already done enough? The man was dead.'

'Because he was guilty!'

'Yes,' Jacob nodded. 'But maybe if I'd been gentler, not so determined to prove him guilty——'

'You know he would have killed himself anyway.' Lori knew that beyond a doubt.

'Perhaps, but he still left you and your mother to the wolves.'

'That's why the truth was never published?' she gasped.

He nodded. 'There seemed no reason to put you and your mother through any more torment. Your father was dead, the bank was happy because they had their money back.' He shrugged. 'That was the end of it.'

'Except that you lost Luke's love and respect because of it!'

His smile faded, the life dying out of his faded eyes. 'It was a price I had to pay.'

'Not any more.' Lori stood up determinedly. 'I may have lost Luke, but I'm going to make sure he isn't lost to *you* any longer. I'm going to tell him the truth——'

'I'd rather you didn't do that,' Jacob interrupted coldly.

'Why not?' her eyes widened.

'Because it's too late for us. I may not be guilty of all Luke believed about me, but I am guilty of a lot of it. I've always been ambitious, your father's case seemed another stepping stone to the top as far as I was concerned, a cut and dried case with the victim having nowhere to run. I'd even got Janet Raynes, your father's mistress—You knew about her?' he frowned worriedly.

She nodded. 'My aunt has just told me everything.'

He touched her hand gently. 'I'm sorry.'

'I'm not. I'm really not.'

Jacob sighed. 'Well, I got Janet Raynes to testify against your father on condition that her charges were kept to a minimum.'

'So that's why she betrayed him!'

He nodded. 'I doubt she would have stood by him, anyway, she wasn't interested if he didn't have the money. No, Janet Raynes was a cold little bitch with an eye to the main chance, and at the time your father was that chance. When he was caught she turned against him immediately. I had no idea what a tragic reaction he would have to knowing she was going to testify against him.'

'Of course you didn't,' Lori assured. 'And Luke has got to be made to understand that.'

He shook his head sadly. 'It really is too late, Lori.'

'Your wife,' she said slowly. 'Did she know the truth? She didn't turn against you too?' she pleaded.

He smiled, love suddenly blazing in the faded grey eyes. 'Barbara—loved me to the end, just as I loved her. Although my son would need convincing of that too,' he added ruefully.

'He's going to get a lot of convincing!' There was a stubborn glint in her eyes.

Jacob touched her hand. 'I'd really like you as my daughter-in-law, Lori.'

'Even knowing about my father?' She looked away.

'You aren't your father,' he assured her. 'Things like dishonesty aren't passed on genetically, no matter what they tell you to the contrary,' he added dryly. 'I'm sorry if Luke and I gave you a rough time last weekend,' he grimaced. 'I'm afraid we bring out the worst in each other. But I would like it if you were to marry him. Do you think you could arrange it?'

She shook her head sadly. 'I'm afraid not.'

His mouth thinned angrily. 'That son of mine is as stubborn as——'

'You are,' Lori smiled.

'Perhaps,' he conceded. 'But you'll visit me again?'

There was an intense sincerity in his voice that convinced her he would really like that. 'I'll try,' she nodded.

It was very late when she arrived back in London, and after all the driving she had done today, the trauma of at last knowing the truth, she was feeling very tired. But not too tired to visit Luke. She was not sure if she could go through with it if she waited until tomorrow. And there was a lonely man in a wheelchair whom she owed this to.

Luke was wearing only a robe when he came to the

door his hair tousled as if from sleep—and yet the deep lines of weariness about his eyes seemed to indicate that, like her, he hadn't been sleeping at all well this last week. His eyes narrowed as he looked at her.

'I'd like to talk to you.' Her words came out fast and determined.

He didn't move. 'It's very late.'

She looked at him unflinchingly, finding only coldness in his face. 'I've just assured your father that it's never too late,' she told him calmly, and watched his start of surprise.

'My father?' he echoed sharply. 'You've been to see my father?'

'Yes.'

'Why?' he rasped.

'Could I come inside, or would you rather we discussed this on the doorstep?' she enquired coolly, confidently. If only she felt that way, but she was a churning bundle of nerves inside!

He flushed at her intended rebuke and stepped back, the tangy smell of his aftershave and the clean smell of his body teasing her senses as she walked past him into the lounge.

'Why did you go to see my father?' he demanded to know.

'Because I needed to know the truth.'

'About what?' he scorned.

'About why he kept quiet about my father, damaged his reputation, gained the disrespect of his son because of his silence. Did *you* ever ask him for the truth, Luke?'

His mouth twisted. 'I already knew it.'

'My father was guilty, I know that now. Aunt Jessie knew the truth all along,' she explained.

'I've already told you, it didn't matter whether your

father was guilty or not.' He moved to the array of bottles on the side, pouring himself a glass of whisky. 'He still caused him to take his own life!'

Lori shook her head. 'You're wrong.'

'No, I'm not.' He threw the whisky to the back of his throat, swallowing deeply, not even flinching at the fiery liquid. 'I don't know what my father has told you, but I should warn you, he's an adept liar. He fooled my mother for thirty-five years——'

Lori's hand moved up to strike him hard across the side of his face, not even flinching at the angry red tide of colour that entered his lean cheeks, the furious glitter of his eyes. 'Pour yourself another drink, Luke,' she advised coldly. 'I think you're going to need it!'

'You little——'

'*Sit down*, Luke,' she instructed angrily. 'And just listen to me for a few minutes!'

'Lori——'

Before he could say any more she began to talk herself, and his angry protests soon trailed off as he listened intently to what she was saying. He sat down on the sofa before she had told him half of what she had learnt today. By the time she had finished she was as pale and worn as he was, the events of the day catching up with her.

'Sit down.' Luke's voice was gentle as he handed her a glass of brandy.

'Thank you.' She sipped at the drink, instantly feeling some of the chill leave her. 'So you see, Luke,' she sighed. 'Your father cared enough not to let the truth be told, even though he knew it would clear him of all the blame in your eyes. And it does clear him, doesn't it, Luke?' She looked up at him anxiously.

'Yes.' His voice was gruff with emotion.

'Thank God for that!' she said shakily.

'Why did you tell me all this, Lori?' He watched her with narrowed eyes.

'To clear your father——'

'No other reason?' he rasped.

She blushed. 'No.'

'None at all?' Luke persisted.

Lori put the glass down and stood up to leave. 'I'd better be going.'

'Didn't you hope that telling me all this would clear up the misunderstanding between us too?' His voice was harsh.

She flinched with reaction. 'No——'

'If you don't say yes, Lori, I swear I'll break your neck!' he told her shakily.

She looked at him with bewildered eyes. 'Luke——!'

'I love you, Lori,' he groaned. 'And I think you really love me too?'

'Yes,' she confirmed breathlessly.

'Your plan backfired on you, didn't it, my darling?' He took her into his arms, his body trembling as he held her close against him. 'You fell in love with me against all the odds.'

She rested her head against his chest. 'Yes.'

'My poor baby,' he caressed the hair at her nape. 'So you gave yourself to me in love.'

'Yes.' She clung to him, hardly able to believe this beautiful dream could be reality.

Luke laughed softly. 'You don't have to say yes all the time, darling.' He cupped her face with his hands, gazing deeply into her eyes. 'I promise not to harm a hair on your beautiful head,' he told her huskily.

Lori swallowed hard. 'I love you.'

He gave a husky groan of triumph, his lips claiming hers in a kiss that seemed to go on and on for ever. 'We'll wipe out the bitterness of the past with our love,

Lori,' he told her between kisses.

'And your father?' Even in her own ecstatic happiness she had to spare a thought for Jacob and the sacrifice he had made all these years.

'I'll go and see him,' Luke nodded.

'Tomorrow,' she urged.

'Well, not tomorrow,' he refused throatily. 'I'll telephone him tomorrow and we'll both go and see him another day. I had other plans for tomorrow.'

'Like what?' she frowned.

'Like making arrangements for us to be married. You will marry me, won't you, Lori?' he sobered.

'Oh yes!' she sighed happily.

'But you won't leave me tonight, will you?' Desire leapt into his eyes like a flame.

She smiled. 'If I don't leave we may never get out tomorrow to buy the licence, and——'

'So we'll go on Tuesday,' he murmured, kissing her deeply.

'Yes,' she groaned, melting against him. 'We'll go on Tuesday. Or maybe Wednesday,' she murmured as she responded to his lips on hers. 'Or Thursday . . .'

ONCE UPON A TIME
IN THE NAME OF LOVE...

...a king gave up his throne. In 1936 King Edward VIII of England (later the Duke of Windsor) rocked the world when he resigned his duties to marry a twice-divorced woman—Wallis Warfield Simpson.

...a famous seventeenth-century English diarist and public official married a fifteen-year-old French girl—who had no dowry. In those days Samuel Pepys's rash decision to marry for love, not money, was unheard-of for a man of his stature and class!

...a seventeenth-century Puritan by the name of John Hutchinson married the woman he adored immediately after her bout with smallpox—despite her horrible disfigurement. None was more surprised than his young bride Lucy Apsley. Even she herself wrote, "All who saw [me] were frightened to look at [me]!"

...a pair of starry-eyed Italian lovers of the thirteenth century risked death at the hands of Gianciotto Malatesta—the young woman's hunchbacked husband—and lost. The ill-fated lovers were Paolo and Francesca, and their tragic story has been immortalized in many literary and artistic works.

...the pretty but indiscreet wife of a prominent British statesman, William Lamb Melbourne, lost everything—her husband, home and reputation—because of her passion for Lord Byron, English romantic poet. It was all for naught, for Lord Byron was a true philanderer and his affair with Lady Caroline Lamb was only one of many.

Yours FREE, with a home subscription to
SUPERROMANCE™

Complete and mail
the coupon below today!

- -

Your FREE gift includes

Anne Mather—Born out of Love
Violet Winspear—Time of the Temptress
Charlotte Lamb—Man's World
Sally Wentworth—Say Hello to Yesterday

FREE Gift Certificate
and subscription reservation

Mail this coupon today!

Harlequin Reader Service

In the U.S.A.
1440 South Priest Drive
Tempe, AZ 85281

In Canada
649 Ontario Street
Stratford, Ontario N5A 6W2

Please send me my 4 Harlequin Presents books free. Also, reserve a subscription to the 8 new Harlequin Presents novels published each month. Each month I will receive 8 new Presents novels at the low price of $1.75 each [*Total—$14.00 a month*]. There are no shipping and handling or any other hidden charges. I am free to cancel at any time, but even if I do, these first 4 books are still mine to keep absolutely FREE without any obligation. **108 BPP CABE**

Offer expires June 30, 1984

NAME	(PLEASE PRINT)

ADDRESS	APT. NO.

CITY

STATE/PROV.	ZIP/POSTAL CODE

If price changes are necessary you will be notified.